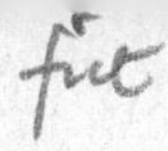

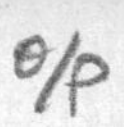

BLIND A[illegible]

GESUALDO BUFALINO was bo[illegible]
1920. He studied literature at Catania and Palermo, and was a teacher by profession, turning author only after his retirement in 1976. He started his first novel, *The Plague-Sower*, in 1950, but it was only in 1981, after taking the discarded manuscript out of the drawer and reworking it, that it was published; it won the Premio Campiello. This has been followed by a succession of remarkable novels and other works, including the present novel, *Blind Argus*. For *Night's Lies*, ("a teasing, calculated, cunning novel" *The Times*), the author won Italy's top literary award, the Strega Prize. A volume of his short stories and his novel *The Plague-Sower* are also to be published by Harvill.

For the translation of *Blind Argus* Patrick Creagh won the John Florio Prize.

By the same author

NIGHT'S LIES

Gesualdo Bufalino

BLIND ARGUS

OR

THE FABLES OF THE MEMORY

Translated from the Italian
by Patrick Creagh

HARVILL
An Imprint of HarperCollins*Publishers*

First published in Italy with the title *Argo il cieco*
by Sellerio editore, Palermo, in 1984
First published in Great Britain
by Collins Harvill in 1989
This edition first published in 1992
by Harvill
an imprint of HarperCollins Publishers,
77/85 Fulham Palace Road,
Hammersmith, London W6 8JB

9 8 7 6 5 4 3 2 1

BRITISH LIBRARY CATALOGUING IN PUBLICATION DATA

Bufalino, Gesualdo
Blind Argus
I. Title II. Argo il cieco. *English*
853'.914 [F]

ISBN 0 00 271048 X

Photoset in Linotron Galliard by
Rowland Phototypesetting Ltd,
Bury St Edmunds, Suffolk

Printed and bound in Great Britain by
HarperCollins Manufacturing, Glasgow

Contents

TO G.

TO HER DELIVERANCE

Arge, iaces, quodque in tot lumina lumen habebas
extinctum est, centumque oculos nox occupat una.

OVID, *Metamorphoses,* I

ZERO

Playbill of purposes. Chapter zero.

"Faintheartedness having lost him the chance to die, an unhappy author resolves to heal himself by writing a happy book. For his material he appeals, as the custom is, to the hundred eyes of memory and the raptures of youth. Except that the further the tale runs on, and prinks itself out with fibs, and teems with fairy lights, the more chinks it leaves between the lines for the chill black present to enter. The author is left with no choice but to defer his return to health until further notice, having rifled his enterprise for some fleeting enticement to embrace the tall story of life . . ."

Start from this premise and see what happens.

ONE

The author, to gladden his thoughts, recalls the old delights of love, and labours lost, in a place that exists no longer.

One summer I was young and happy, in 'Fifty-One. Neither before nor after: just that summer. It may have been by grace and favour of the place I lived in, a town like a pomegranate split in two, close to the sea yet pastoral, the one half clinging to a cliff-face, the other bespattered at its foot, with innumerable flights of steps like peacemakers between the two and clouds in the sky, between one bell-tower and the next, as breathless as couriers of the King's Light Cavalry . . . What a fluttering there was at that time, of linen sheets and muslins for trousseaux, up and down the alleyways of the two Módicas, the Upper and the Lower. And what angel girls dangled over the window-sills, each and every one of them raven-haired. The one I loved was the raven of them all.

I was a rotten dancer in 'Fifty-One. Not that I'd ever danced well from the start. All the same, I had made some headway in the figured tangos and the polkas, and only blundered in the twirly bits. Whereas now that from both the Americas new dances with new names were disembarking every day by the dozen, I practised to the best of my ability in front of the mirror in my boarding-house, whistling a despondent accompaniment. I say, I did my best . . . On the dance-floors, in the dance-halls, wherever I chanced to snap my scissor-legs at random, all the smiles and plaudits of August were for someone else: Liborio Galfo, the virtuoso of the boogie-woogie.

Oh well, I was then about thirty, give or take a year, and for reasons known to myself I had never been twenty. I was twenty now, out of the blue, that summer's gift to me. After all, I was owed it.

Now I won't have any old French wiseacre coming to me and saying you aren't happy at twenty, however tardily and make-believe you reach that age. Even if you love (though she loves you not) a raven-haired, olive-skinned lass with a snake-hips physique and a voice that croons *booo-karooo booo-karooo* in the groves of her throat. Even if she has naught but scorn for the lisping, myopic poet, and reserves the flash of her eyes exclusively for the opposition. No, you are not unhappy, however vociferously you claim to be so, and though every other Saturday, (and every other one as well), back home from frolics at Cava d'Aliga, you have a good cry before dropping off and sleeping twelve hours at a stretch. You weep, you sleep, you dream. And in your dreams you eat your rivals alive, ruffle their curly locks at will, and their Musketeer moustachios, and mangle the creases in their spinning trousers. It takes very little in a dream, in the midst of a pirouette, to lay a gunpowder plot, to slip beneath that gliding heel the irresistible banana-skin . . .

Unrequited loves, believe me, are the most expedient. They have none of that taste of vinegar and ashes that accompanies ephemeral unisons. Some of this I learnt from books, the rest I kidded myself into believing, out of shyness, the sulks, or priggish vanity. So I didn't try to make a hit with this girl, or become chummy. "I love her, but that's nothing to do with her. It's entirely my business," I announced to myself one Sunday while shaving in the bathroom, and the dictum appealed to me. I scrawled it with a fingertip on the steamed-up mirror, and it pleased me ever after to repeat it as an antidote to the vipers of jealousy. Maria Venera felt nothing for me? So much the better. This gave me infinite freedom. What I felt for her was mine and mine alone, and in fantasy I could toy with her and conquer her to my heart's content.

Even if I had to cheat. We all know that the most exquisite of pleasures is cheating oneself at patience. In any case, if someone had asked me how many times I had attempted to pierce her indifference, I would have answered with a shrug. Or, perhaps, I might have admitted that I'd once asked her to dance a dizzying *Blue Danube*, and reduced her poor feet to toads beneath the harrow; and that later, at the buffet, while she was sipping a liqueur, I had mumbled something about her having lovely hair, and in return received an ironic curtsey. And I might have confessed that for a whole month I had waited for her every evening and followed her home, only to hide in the end in the dark of a doorway. And lastly, to make a clean breast of it, that I had written her poems. These I would solemnly declaim in the twilight before going downstairs into the street, while I was still dawdling, peeping through the slats of the shutters down into the Corso (which they called the "Salon" – a majestic tide of stone slabs between two wide-flung pavements), waiting for the town lights to come on, and the commencement, with all the ritual of a princely Court of Love, of the public promenade.

Thanks to the tinkle of some arcane alarm-clock in my head, the same that during my schooldays sprang my eyes open at one minute to seven, I already knew at what moment and abreast of which shop I would pass her and blushingly greet her with my eyes. I would make a guess at which dress she'd be wearing: the black with the braid and the lace collar, or the black with the basques below the waist, or the beaded black so clinging about the bosom that it winded me. Did I say I'd guess? Easy enough. Maria Venera never wore anything but black, except on truly festive occasions, when she was to be seen advancing beneath the lamplight swathed in white plissé, and white in the face herself from the thousand expectations of God knows what that pressed upon her heart . . .

Unrequited loves? Great God deliver us! A murrain on the man who says they're the most expedient! You chew the cud of rancour, rave over fantasies and phantoms, talk off the top of your head and succumb to the mildest of bacteria. And heaven be praised if it doesn't all come to a bad end. For love is such a strange bird, such a gypsy child, that you can't, you can't . . . I tell you that when she sang the *Habanera* at the piano, Maria Venera transfixed my heart with all the seven holy hatpins!

Maria Venera had this piano, you see, one of the few relics of erstwhile prosperity; for she was a poor girl now, an only daughter, and an orphan, reduced to living alone with her grandfather and relying for holidays on the goodwill of the Trubias, aunts on her mother's side. She could scarcely wait for summer to come, to pack her bags and turn her back on the doors of the old palazzo; a crumbling edifice, but none the less intimidating, smothered as it was with gentilitial fripperies, from the sculpted pediments to the baroque grotesques forming the corbels of the balconies. I passed the palazzo every day of the week, and my strategy was to stop, pencil and pad in hand, as if making a sketch or taking a note. Every so often I would nod, with the grave air of a student or a scholar observing the stony grimaces of the place, the comical plug-uglies with the loutish snouts of infuriated fiends, whom I dubbed with names from my schooldays: Barbariccia, Calcabrina, Alichino, and all the rest of Dante's devilry. In their gaping mouths the moss ran riot.

To tell the truth, the place was enough to make you weep, mortified as it was by time, and by neglect. Only the stone, where the stucco had peeled away, was lovely and chaste and naked as a seashell. Quick, should the sunset strike it, to flush like a cheek. It was limestone from illustrious quarries, quarried for heraldic houses. Heraldic also was Maria Venera, one such as is sent from our part of the world to study at the Conservatoire in Palermo. Whence, prematurely, she returned, following the death of her parents and the squandering of the property, though retaining a gentle, waning remembrance of those studies, the effects of which came to our ears on evenings of sultry sirocco, when from the open window, surging in billows down towards the church of the Carmine, and towards San Giorgio, and the Twelve Holy Apostles on the steps of San Pietro, we heard the schoolgirl pot-pourri from *Carmen* (Maria Venera, wherever thou art, blessèd be thy name!).

This grandfather of hers was Alvise, Don Alvise Salibba, and he was going on for ninety. He had been at one time a splendour of a fellow, and so he still was in his way. He waggishly blamed his extravagantly non-Sicilian name on a bygone honeymoon in Venice during which, one night, his mother had swopped her husband (laid low by rheumatism) for a certain Alvise, blue-eyed gondolier, and nine months later had given the name an encore in the Register of Births, in recognition and fond remembrance . . . Just another of the cynical, titillating yarns with which the old man loved to stun the passers-by as he sat, on the folding stool he carried about under his arm, beneath a benjamin-tree in the avenue, right opposite the Conservative Club, where he had sworn never to set foot again after losing his last farm in a gambling binge. So there he would sit in panama and spats, summer and winter alike, hooking with the crook of his walnut stick at any ankles in transit, whether of friends, acquaintances, or mere tourists, and hauling them hungrily to him, ordaining a halt and a hearing. Little by little a circle would form, for Alvise had the gift of the gab . . . and the days were so languorous then, there was so much light in the air, and in that light it was a fine thing to stand and listen to a venerable elder, solemnly hoary with years, discoursing of Lina Cavalieri and La Bella Otero.

Alvise had known them all, he assured us, in the days of his youth, as he toured Europe in a Hispano-Suiza, with a chauffeur from Ragusa Ibla and a polyglot chef lured by the chink of silver from the Grimaldi court at Monte Carlo. His stories, fragrant with eau-de-cologne and cigar smoke, embraced all the celebrities and legends of a lifetime more remote from us than that of a denizen of Golconda or Samarkand, and wooingly they made us children again. He himself, let it be said, kept a brave flag flying in the wind, if there was truth in the rumour that until very recently he had required that his bed – and not simply as a warming pan – should contain his sixty year-old serving-woman.

He would talk, would Alvise, and his voice lent spice to the light refracted by the stones of the buildings and the churches, both the white and the honey-coloured, becoming a compelling oracle which the last century had faithfully preserved for us. It was of rare quality, the light in Módica, during those Junes and Julys of 'Fifty-One: a mote-filled lucency I have never since seen the like of, which I recall as coming in soft puffs, rather like the Holy Ghost, through the dangling chains of the fly-screen in the doorway of Don Cesare's trattoria, and curling in golden aureoles around the flanks of the wine-flasks. Here in this place even the grease-stains and blotches on the flowered oilcloth consented to fashion the alphabets of kindly language, and murmured a loving word. Although the truly enchanted spot was further towards the back, in a nook of the kitchen, on a soot-black trestle where the fishtank rested. Hither the eyes of the customers were drawn at five-minute intervals, for the wriggles of the prisoner within seemed, in their apparent randomness, to create a pattern of songs without sound, alternately veiling, and revealing, the celestial intrigues of the season.

Insensitive to sophistry, blind to all mystery, Don Cesare busied himself with strewing the aquarium with crumbs gathered from between the plates, not omitting to bugle a military "Come to the Cookhouse Door", which he claimed was perfectly familiar to every sea-creature from mullet to mermaid. He was echoed by the cook, Mariccia, or Amapola – we may choose between her real name and her other, the *nom de guerre* from her times of greatest glory, when she landed up in Benghazi as a camp-follower, an amatory mercenary, and on one occasion found herself in a thirty-roomed Alhambra tiled with *azulejos* from floor to ceiling, and in the midst of it a gigantic four-poster surrounded by fountains of sweet-scented water. In this Thousand-and-One-Nights setting, with the aid of an impuberal Arab girl, it had been her lot to face a savage three-cornered session with a uniformed Fascist official, probably some bearded impostor, claiming to be called Italo (what! the Military Governor?) who had the two of them lash him in turn with his great leather belt.

Ah, those were the days! By this time Mariccia was worn out and querulous, with wobbly teeth and the vapours. Of bygone joustings of the flesh she had only a misty recollection, such as a retired bosun, seated on a bench at the dockside, might recapture of the shipwrecks of his youth. But she was a good soul, Amapola, and thanks to kind heart and good sense had retained a sympathy and a benevolent enthusiasm which she was obliged to vent in thrills and throbs and gasps of agitation and astonishment, sometimes over the pages of pre-war adventure stories, which she hoarded in the luggage that had seen so many lifetimes; on other, and far preferable, occasions by listening to my outpourings in praise of Maria Venera. For on the subject of that girl the words gushed from me in torrents every day. Out loud to Mariccia, and back home, with pen and paper, in jubilant effusions which I tacked to the wall with four drawing-pins and then committed to memory, as the topographies of banks are studied by apprentice cracksmen.

I was teaching at a girls' school then, in this town which was not my own town, boarding out with a certain Widow Amalia (her daughter was away at school), and weekly beneficiary of her libidinous pinguitudes. From which on each occasion I departed more contrite, eager to hurry to my room and do penance by writing about the other one. More fool me if I forgot to lock the door, and the widow, stealing stealthily up from her little bookshop on the ground floor, caught me red-handed with pen couched at the ready, heart and mind in ferment, and the tears on the cheeks. I always wept buckets when I wrote love-poems.

So eventually I took to going to the bar, to ensconce myself at a table I could call my own, from which, if I glanced up, the obliging and manifold blandishments of the town movie-show unrolled before my eyes. For me there was no better work-table, or grandstand, or salon, or occasion for companionship. No better distraction from lovesickness. It might be a visit from the trumpeter in the town band, who loved to flaunt his prowess even off duty, and invigoured by the pantomime of my applause would sally with all the fervour of a guardsman to storm the most unassailable heights . . . Or then again, along would come the town loonies, all of them sweet and peaceful, each with some lonesome fancy in his heart, to which I alone offered credence and comfort . . . Or else, as they strolled arm in arm, I'd be waved a greeting by the two friends and rival witches, Donna Tònchila Cangiula and 'gna Ninfa Scacciaguerra, at whose doors I was destined to knock later on, anxious less for their suffumigations and sorceries than for their cheerfully funereal banter.

Most especially (of my everyday friends I will tell you later) I relished the company of those who professed less prosaic trades, of Carmine *'u ciarmavermi*, vendor of seaweeds to cure the worms in children, of Cicirè the marriage-broker, of the Malanova brothers, snappers-up of votive offerings and rag-and-bone men . . .

A stage-set was this town, a theatre of rose-tinted stones, a carnival of marvels. And how the jasmine breathed at the fall of evening! Oh to praise her for ever, to rediscover my own image in such a fond mirage of distances . . . To see myself there as I went out of a morning to meet with the tumble of life, wide open to the whole of life, to the rolling of its dice and prodigalities of laughter and tears . . . and to the symphonies of bells. What grand chiming there was in Módica in those days, for weddings and for christenings, vespers and angelus, but most of all for funerals, they did so much dying in Módica; so that every half-hour, and no one turned a hair, you heard the air cloven by the silvery, encouraging ding-dong of death.

Oh to praise her for ever . . . For then I was an aging child, aged by years and by books, but a child for all that. As you can but be if you wake in the morning and open your wide eyes wide and brimming with wonder.

TWO

Litany of lovely nights. And how we came to that summer by way of different seasons and various corrugations of feeling.

Happiness, my bygone skies; nights, my paradise . . .

Indigo silences of the newborn night, when through the flimsy screen of walls, rising from the roadway to your pillow, though swiftly dwindling and dying, comes the footstep of a lonely walker (roving drunkard, home-going midwife, zealous cut-purse, Friday-night adulterer), setting a seal on the day as a hand at the end of a drama softly lowers a curtain . . .

Black cloak of one in the morning, latent with serenades . . . In which, should voices sound, they seem to be muffled by subtle mutes; unless it be a confabulation of ghosts on a bench down there, among the flowerbeds around the ubiquitous War Memorial . . .

(Have you noticed how from afar each word comes disembodied, mingled with all sorts of other sounds? The dripple of the fountains, the servants going about their tranquil tasks, a puff of wind between the houses . . .)

So you get out of bed, you prick up your ears. Beneath the bare soles of your feet the wrinkles in the floor-bricks are of a poignant coolness. Before you have time to push ajar a shutter it is too late, below there is left only soot-black silence, deepest of silences. Lean out, and there's only a little beastie, a witch's furry familiar, glimpsed crossing the road on felt-pad paws, leaving the stones for an instant phosphored with nomad eyes, a transient zigzag.

Nights, nights flush with summer, as we stroll home from La Sorda after the party, and over the landscape of carobs and olives a crescent moon still hangs, marbling it with patches of light as white as a young nun's habit. And the couples, the girls arm in arm with their sweethearts, fashion weird elongated dance-patterns between the thickets, enlacing and loosing, in a to and fro of sweet satisfaction which, at the edge of town, frays out into chatter and goodnights and stealthy endearments of hands. And the Terrible Mothers waiting at the window feel a mild fuzz of sleep enfeebling them into forgiveness . . .

O girls, I loved you! Maria Venera, Angela, Ines . . . Even today, at times, a wait at a level-crossing is enough, when it's raining and the train seems lost in the dark, though a couple of whistles had given me hopes that it was near at hand, and the miniature, glistening grin of the car radio drowses me, lulls me, beguiles me into one of my recurrent ecstasies of daydreaming. . . A ten-minute wait is enough, plus the pandering fingertips of the rain palping the windscreen, plus the liquorice of that sax mid-way between Hilversum and Monteceneri. There now! Through the mishmash of sounds I slice a misty peep-hole at which, one after the other, all the girls of my life appear . . . Summers of yesteryear, hillside pergolas, pathways winding among dwarf pear-trees, the strand at Pietranera . . . A raised hand brandishes a sandal gritty with yellow sand. A fiery enormous cloud flares up . . . now it is swarming with dark rafts. Oh indeed it is true, as the fellow said, that the ball I tossed up as a child in the park has not yet fallen to earth. And wee silly secrets are concealed again on the gummy side of postage stamps; a trinket snaps, rolls under a chest-of-drawers . . . Bloodless sickles of lips, melodies of past pavanes . . . Venera, Assunta, Isolina, you bevies of roses, last word in trepidation! Where are you now, *belles d'antan*? Where is Flora *la belle Romaine*, or Thaïs, or Adalgisa the toffee-nosed cashier at the "Cinema Splendide"? Where is she now, and with how many offspring, and crow's-feet and wrinkled neck, and varicose veins on those plump, unforgettable calves . . . And my silk tie with the green elephants and pagodas, is it now a kitchen rag? Do we find it stopping a bung-hole? *Eheu, fugaces, Postume, Postume* is my grammar-school grumble . . . and along with Posthumus I think of Proust. For in fact and in truth, all the voices and the faces of my women, all added up, weigh scarcely as much as a scruple of dust, and neckties and cashiers are fleeting things, alas; as are the years.

Yes, but what a pleasure to sit here all the same, here in the driver's seat, with the waft of the heater comforting my old shins. How senseless and pleasant it is, Venera, Ada, Corrada, to invite you to a pow-wow here before me! Here on this misted video I see you bloom, and wilt, and bloom again with every swish of the windscreen-wiper . . . Until the goods-train looms, blind and gross, sending you all ascatter across the landscape, leaving behind, in its grey stench of dog, only a spray of raindrops and that momentary flicker like a fairground light, or a glow-worm unwittingly pulverized underfoot . . .

The other three seasons, before that summer, had flitted swiftly by, neither happy nor sad. Autumn occasionally brought us a gauze of mist outside the classroom windows, and caused the most horsy of horseflies to expire, pawing the air, between two pages of the class-register. The last fig of October, puckered with sweetness, remained unpicked at the tip of a chill-stiffened branch. Nothing left in the fields but the dead-heads of cardoons, bolt upright like a melancholy platoon of Capuchin skeletons. Then the mulberries in the courtyards lost their leaves, it started to rain every day from half-past eight till nine, apparently on purpose, as if the stars were envious of the first country outing of the school year, forever promised and forever deferred.

The girls would arrive with a slender bundle of books hanging from the little fingers of their right hands, hoping to dump them on the desk and to set off at once in crocodile up the ramps of Monserrato. Fond hopes indeed! Scarcely had they sighted the main door before they heard the voice of headmaster Biscari intoning the old proverb he had adopted as a kind of perennial, affectionate tease: "Mackerel skies bring buckets of schoolwork." And their chagrin was complete if, eyes raised in viperine reproaches against the intimidations of the heavens, a gust of north wind took them unawares without respecting, sad to say, their modesty. The esoteric petticoats of age eighteeen were hoisted like pennants and astonished the world. And that fleeting moment brought to light certain morsels of unpredictably plump flesh, divulged certain glorious gulfs of shadow, knickers sometimes not exactly vestal . . .

At last, at the head of the steps appeared Ermenegilda and she might have been Pallas Athene! Ermenegilda the caretaker, tall, imposing, stern and queenly, made an imperious sign for her people to enter. With the rain already pelting down, in single file, breasts borne bashfully between a double row of ready elbows, in streamed the unruly rabble, pouring on my timorous, untamed heart the dark resin of their glances.

"Oh that I might come to you, belovèd,
Like a thief, so that it would not seem . . ."

I began, profiting from the momentary silence which followed the roll-call; but, far from following me, no one appeared even to be listening. They were all shooting furious sidelong glances through the window, where the air was growing light in the nine-fifteen sunshine, while a satirical sunbeam broke through the storm and danced around the classroom.

"Buckets of schoolwork," then . . . But they were distracted by the least trifle from the street below: the flirtatious tootle of a bus-horn, more or less insistent according to the petulance and youth of the driver. Or else, after the tapping of rain on the window-panes, the other, not dissimilar tapping, of sparrows more anxious for shelter than curious about the poetry of Pier delle Vigne. Or again, it might be the pattern of my tie, and whether on one shoulder, among accumulated drifts of dandruff, there dangled, or did not dangle, a long sleek hair belonging, they reckoned, to someone other than me. And then I realized that the seasonal arpeggios of tears were due to begin, the sudden burying of faces and tresses in the crooks of arms: the tears of each summer-holiday lately-jilted heart; of each fresh Octobrine budding bride, but glum already with misunderstandings and tantrums; of each Plain Jane of a swot condemned to the solitude of top-of-the-class; of each dowerless dream-girl with no dress to flaunt next New Year's Eve; and of all the others who sobbed away in emotion and emulation . . .

In contrast I pondered on my own lofty sentiments of love, so infinitely more adult, and was happy to have schooled them into a comatose condition. Here was I, self-contained, cossetting my own figments and fancies; there was she, Maria Venera, behind her bulwark of intransitive hauteur and baronial stones. I pondered . . . and the pentameters of the poets died on my lips. The pause enabled me, among the whisperings of two chatterboxes taken unawares by the sudden armistice, to catch the tail-end of a syllable they had not managed to bite off in time – the end of an adjective that could only apply to a young man, or to a dress.

And so on and so forth, week after week, while the weather turned visibly more sombre and a chill crept in. My thermometer was my coat-collar, pulled further up about my ears each break-time as I made a dash for a cup of something at the Caffè Bonaiuto, buffeted by the gusts hurled from hilltop to hollow, from the spur of rock above us, bald bird with outspread wings, guardian of the unchanging ceremonies of the town. From now on we could rest assured of the vesperal aroma of roasting chestnuts, and would beg sleep from the hiss of tyres on wet tarmac. From the teachers' common-room we would become used to seeing the news-stand opposite all sodden and dripping with rain; and, a step beyond, the giant *pissoir* on the pavement, offering itself to the forays of the wind like a roofless ruin at Herculaneum or Pompeii. Maybe I, an outsider, only I, would stick it out on the evening of the Fair, I and nobody else, playing "she loves me, she loves me not" by potting clay pipes with a pistol in a deserted shooting gallery.

*

November, December, the last wet dribbles of Nineteen-Fifty. Winter is now at its height, deadly melancholy with ice and floods and cats with hazel-nut eyes . . . My birthday passed without any presents, though I would never have expected them from my friends and colleagues, who were also exiles from home and eking out meagre wages. But nonetheless ready to devise sprees and student pranks, desperate remedies costing twopence-worth of imagination. I was fond of these lads, but of an afternoon I preferred the cinema, those smashing Warner Bros shoot-'em-ups with the stars I loved best, the lovelies of the B-Features – Ann Sheridan, Ida Lupino . . . Or in the evening, the recitals at the Philharmonic Society, all weepy Chopin (especially the piece where you hear the drop, drop, drop) beneath the dauntless digits of Maestra Tuvè, yellow with nicotine and knobbly as drumsticks.

I never missed one of these gatherings, even on wet windy evenings, when I was forced to appear in public with floppy galoshes and chapped lips, ludicrously smeared with vaseline (I have always suffered acutely from the least nip of cold). For there before me, in the front row, seated on a cane chair, was a certain Maria Venera, knees pressed tight together beneath her pleated skirt, hands clasped in her lap, and wearing the frown of a reputed connoisseur, rigid from the waist up like a bust of Nefertiti on a plinth in the museum.

When I emerged, if the rain had stopped I would be met by my sneering, melophobic mates. I had no choice but to join them for an aimless stroll through the obscurèd purlieus. Off we went then, vagrant and muffled up in our turned overcoats, me with disgruntled acquiescence in the most mutton-headed fatuities, such as smearing foul filth on the doorknobs of the nobs, or shadowing the election billstickers, grabbing any momentarily abandoned bag and muddling up the tops and bottoms of the posters, so that what got on to the walls was a jumble of sickles, crosses, hammers and what not, pasted together at random. At which point I would turn and fall ("What, even *you*, professore!") into the scandalized embrace of Miciacio the night-watchman. Or else we might pass ourselves off as surveyors from Palermo, reporting on dilapidated buildings. We would steer through many a narrow bosphorus – Via Sant'Acconsio, Ronco Albanese – where the space between the humble, one-storey *dammusi* is little more than a passageway, and from the glowing ovens wafts a fetching aroma of baking sardines. We would crack up drainage projects, restorations . . . and when we left we were followed by a male chorus of astonishment and benediction, and now and again, from the women, a temptress glance . . .

That's how they were, these friends of mine. They were fresh from the war, and to help them forget it they played cruel games, like children. Saro Licausi, Pietro Iaccarino . . . shades, today . . .

I lost a romantic bet with Saro Licausi: who could spot and pick the first almond blossom upon the slopes of Idria, where we went every Sunday. He was set on winning, even to the ruin of a pair of shoes, and scrambled up as wary as a poacher to where he thought he had discovered the most generous tree. And there in the thicket of twigs he was granted an impalpable pearl, a rose-tinted dewdrop, a hesitant fritillary scarcely budding on a branch after a night of lightning incubation.

I lost, but I never paid up. We used to bet on everything in those days, but no one ever forked out. Now that the weather was taking a turn for the better we used to go flower-hunting, and they taught me the names: "This is an anemone, this is an azalea." But I baptized each flower with the name of a girl in 4B, whereas at school, vice versa, I gave a flower-name to every girl in the class, in the budding swell of her school overalls.

And now overnight on the roofs the pigeons multiplied, until the sacristan's volleys of stones could scarcely miss them. The sky was already quite another thing, a porcelain sky overflowing with light like an over-full pitcher groaning to disgorge it; to pour out light at random into any nearby orifice or aperture, be it throat of skylark or belfry clamoured with bells. There were more or less a hundred churches in Mòdica, and as many bell-towers, from San Pietro to San Giuseppe and the church of the Gesù . . . A hundred churches, each with the breath of its faithful kneaded into the plaster as the smell of a workman's sweat will cling to his dungarees. Fine, carnal, baroque churches with full, rounded columns like the moulded legs of Maria Venera, churches with domes and with cupolas which, if they reminded my friends of the shape of cakes of warm grape-must in Caltagirone bowls, in me they aroused another and more touching similitude: the pearly breasts of Maria Venera within her half-unbuttoned bodice . . .

Easter fell early that year, and to make their *cassatas* they had to look snappy to lay in cheese and ricotta from the shepherds up on the plateau. With the worst will in the world our *patron* Don Cesare set off in a one-horse jalopy, returning with bootsoles redolent of sheep and cattle droppings, while in addition (he complained) his nostrils still smarted from the stench of 'gna Tura, a sun-scorched shepherdess notorious in those parts for the sexual tax she exacted from any male wayfarer who chanced upon her.

But at last, from the ridges of Monte Tabbuto to the grottoes of Pantálica and Íspica, the whole earth, Miocene and Pliocene, schists, faults, seedbeds and burrows, veins of water and seismic crevices, all the land of the Val di Noto trembled, and little by little spread her limestone lips into a smile. Between two stones a scorpion rubbed his sleepy two pincers together; from the fortress of a clump of grass a cheeky little lizardess poked out her snout for a moment, pulled it in, poked it out. Don Alvise peeled off his long woollen longjohns and lo! it was spring.

THREE

Flight of the girl and farce of her retrieval.

Spring in a manner of speaking, for spring in a minute is summer – no lukewarm land is this! Not a second to wean the sun before he's up and roaring. The same with the girls: yesterday you saw them children, you chucked them under the chin; but today two metal-tipped nipples thrust at their blouses, and beneath their brows smoulder two sultry eyes.

From now on, in Módica, who gets a wink of sleep? One evening, serenade after serenade, guitars and mandolins, lapping at the balconies; the next night everyone off to Donnalucata to buy fish straight off the boats; another, with bloodshot eyes and disappointed fingers, alas, parading deceptive aces in a poker game . . . Just as well the nights only lasted a jiffy, puffs of black smoke between the amethyst embers of evening and the white torch of dawn . . .

On such a night as this Maria Venera ran away from home, and at midnight of that same night, historically speaking, began my fabled season of happiness.

It happened that Iaccarino and I were seated after dinner at the chessboard (no cards that evening, thank goodness). Just the two of us at this point, since Madama Amalia had gone to bed a while before, leaving behind her the odour of anti-mosquito coils. Iaccarino was carrying on in his usual way, partly to relieve boredom and partly to harass me while I was plotting my moves: "Avaunt, thou varlet!" said he. "Beg for clemency!" Or else, musingly, "I feel superfluous this evening. A sty, a mote in the eye of the Creator. I'm swiping your pawn . . ."

Of the two colleagues I have mentioned, Pietro Iaccarino, poet, philosopher, already forty, was my friend of friends. Something, perhaps, both less and more than a friend; a kind of thoroughly unfaithful double. Because, if in one way he echoed some of my fits of moodiness and lightning schizophrenias, in others there was no companionship more incongruous than ours; between him, man of intellect, mountebank and lampoonist, and me, man of sentiment, wedded to the lonely vice of dream and daydream. Nor would we have found any way of becoming reconciled, him and me, had we not tacitly chosen to play upon our common love of reading, our taste for puns, nonsenses, and erudite jokes and jargon, monks and moonlighters of books as we both professed to be. It was no coincidence, that whereas Licausi preferred the hotel, we had landed up as tenants of Madama's, more to wear out the chairs, perhaps, in the ground-floor bookshop, than the mattresses above-stairs. Iaccarino in particular, ever since they had put him on the permanent staff and no longer hurled him from school to school the length and breadth of the country, had taken up fixed abode in the bookshop, browsing there as in a brothel, without, to the best of my remembrance, having spent more than a couple of coins for a thriller to read on the train. And what's more, mutilating it – *rip*! – of the last chapter, so as to leave the name of the culprit in the air. With a view, in his own words, of guaranteeing him an escape hatch in a world where all is expiated, from high treason to a parking fine.

He had taken to Madama at once, it was friendship at first sight, though jeopardized by his endless jibes and her counterattacks; *she* scolding him for drinking and talking too much, *he* in return saying he did it to avoid listening to *her*. With the result that sometimes, when things were dicey between them, I would see him hanging around in the street, waiting for the widow to withdraw to her own quarters and leave the coast clear. Only then would he decide to push the door ajar, reconnoitre with his nose and, as if addressing the most indolent of errand boys, invite me to a game of chess at the table of the dear departed. He would plump himself down opposite me, gaunt, olive-skinned, and stick a pair of thick glasses onto his boxer's nose; a nose for which it was never known who was the more to blame, a clumsy midwife or the fist of a pugnacious husband. A nose which was the cross he had to bear and never ceased complaining about ("Call this a face? Why, it's a gas-mask!"). Between one move and the next he blamed it for his failure to become a filmstar, or comic foil to Luigi Cimara, but above all for the few rebuffs he had suffered in the course of his long soldiering as a philanderer. As he described the latter, it sounded more epic than a Napoleonic campaign, but in truth it must have been consummated in a few swift skirmishes in any available cubby-hole, at the expense of some spinsterish secretary, vintage colleague, or freckled supply-teacher. He reeled off the catalogue, caring not a hoot for my resolute inattention, though he paid me back by plunging a drowsy head down among the pawns when it was my turn to retaliate by singing him my psalm of unrequited love. Which that evening froze on my lips. *That* evening, half-way through our game, Don Alvise burst into the room, throwing open the door with the air of a bass catching tenor and soprano in the very act. We needed no explanations: it was clear at once that if the old man was out at that time of night with neither hat nor stick, his face as ashen-coloured as potters' clay, and his only answer to our questioning looks an epilepsy of the hands, then something pretty serious must have happened to him, worthy of an urgent S.O.S. Iaccarino and I were at his side at a bound, just in time to prop him up while Madama, summoned at the tops of our voices, dashed to his aid with smelling-salts, her clothing in spirited disarray, and lowered him into the nearest chair, not without first relieving his scrawny neck of its black silk cravat.

When he was able to speak, Alvise astonished us. For in his voice, along with the indignation that sent it shooting into falsetto, no doubt about it there gurgled a bubble of laughter. Enough to make us think that what he was about to say tickled him as much as it tormented him; or at any rate that the mishap, coming at him point-blank, had indeed bowled him over at first, but had very soon converted him into a twitching puppet.

"Liborio Galfo!" he began. "That pickled sprat, that quivering prick! And I say no more out of respect for our good lady . . ."

At this Madama, suspecting sarcasm, began to bridle, but he silenced her with a gesture of impatience.

"A fellow with no punch in his pants," he continued, swivelling to right and to left the moist blue puddles he had instead of eyes. "And from Lower Módica, too!" He repeated this as if he could not credit it, or as if we had contradicted him. And here he stopped, unexpectedly reached into his waistcoat pocket, pulled out an enormous fob-watch, and began to wind it.

"What's he done to you?" I asked cautiously, uncertain whether this was the right question. The reply was immediate, and hurled me into the blackest desolation.

"What's he done to me? What have *they* done, you mean! They've eloped, that's what! Hee hee . . ." And he started again with his tummy-rumblings of testy laughter, keeping it up so long that the others (not I) felt obliged to join in for the sake of good manners: Once under way, he lost no time in describing the discovery: how after a couple of hours' sleep he had happened to wake up because of the heat, he who always went to bed at nine and slept like a log; how he had gone onto the terrace for a breath of air and, to his horror, seen the Topolino belonging to that fellow, the dancing-man, down there in front of the main entrance, with the engine running and the door flung wide; and how an instant later, before he caught on and was able to let out a yell, he saw the girl, a suitcase in either hand, climb into the car and vanish thunderously into the darkness. It was vital to pursue them at once, avert the scandal and rescue (though he doubted she was in danger from a Simple Simon such as *that*) a famous virginity.

I heard it, and my cheeks were aflame with jealousy. I kept telling myself that I ought not to care, but it took me aback all the same to think of Maria Venera in the hands of that brilliantined jumping-gigolo. One thing to remember her mettlesome and radiant in his arms for a waltz; quite another to imagine her hobnobbing with him in a bedsome nook, amid downy nuptial ardours. So this nervous spasm of envy, chicken-hearted hero though I be, made me the first to want to get moving. The neighbour who had given Alvise a lift down had already left, but Iacca's little car stood at the street door. As the flight had most likely headed north, we put our trust in God and took the main road to Noto.

This blind pursuit along the fast straights awarded us no excitement other than to think that every red dot appearing or disappearing in front of us was the tail-light of the fugitives, be it lamp of noctambulant cart or bivouac of migratory pickpocket. I was at the wheel, on the understanding that Iaccarino would take over for the return journey; and I drove hell-for-leather. It was a bend that betrayed me. We skidded, the car turned over twice, and by some miracle ended the right way up, but jammed against a kerbstone. I knew nothing of all this. At the first shock a mountain, Pelion certainly, but probably Ossa as well, had fallen on my head.

When I came to and discovered, by groping around the *opus incertum* of my face, that no serious damage had been done, even before I opened my eyes I felt the uninjured breath of my two companions on my brow, and managed just in time to choke back the invocation that was already clamouring upon my lips: "Venera, Venera! . . ."

With their help I tried getting to my feet. No broken bones, so "Up boys and at 'em!" However, no such thing was needed. Iaccarino pointed to the sign of a wayside inn a few yards ahead, and beside it, under a brushwood pergola masquerading as a garage, the motionless posterior of the car we were after. Thank God, then, for the accident, without which we would have raced on by.

At the sight of it my strength returned, but with it came a stab of apprehension about the hair-raising scene in store for me, the *consummatum est* of the pair of them in the hotel, the fly in the ointment, the earwig on the rose. As we approached, however, I was reassured by a lighted window on the second floor, and the dance music floating down from it, sounding to my ears like an angel's dulcimer: if they hadn't put out the light, and were listening to songs on the radio, perhaps the worst had not yet happened. It was therefore not without hope that I stood waiting until the door opened to our knocking and the landlord's face peered out. I recognized it at first glance, having met it as a boy in the illustrations to *Treasure Island.* Only then he was called Long John Silver, and combined a black eye-patch with the scar on his lip and piratical peg-leg . . . We rushed him, we were already on the stairs, making for the *Surriente d'e' 'nnamur-ate* that flowed from the closed door, and . . . what a spectacle, when Iacca and I had barged the door down, was the Philippi between Venera and Alvise; Venera, still fully dressed, purring on the naked chest of her abductor, who was seated on the sofa; Alvise, panting from rage and effort, with a furious strap in his hand and a wheeze of laughter in his gullet . . . Having choked this down, and rolling savage eyes as in a silent movie, he bore down on them for all the world like a concrete-mixer.

Galfo got to his feet beneath the blows, putting up no fight but backing towards the door where, however, Iaccarino barred his way, lapideous and valiant as Leonidas at Thermopylae. Xerxes thrust him aside with one arm and sent him sprawling, after which, without a word, shirt in hand, quick march out at the stage door. There remained the girl, standing haughtily entrenched behind the radio console which, as though nothing had happened, went on singing. But I, at this point, made the great gesture, interposed myself between the lash and her, absorbed the last blow on my nose and, flinging an arm round her waist, dragged her off; she was suddenly tearful.

As we passed the limping landlord, flabbergasted but none the less keen to press a charge for damages, I was startled to see on his shoulder, more Stevensonian still, a prattling parrot whose parting insult we all, out of sheer good manners, chose to ignore.

*

On the way back, while Alvise sat in silence beside Iaccarino, I had the luck to be in the back seat, enjoying the warmth of the girl against my left side. Like secret messages I felt the desultory sharps and flats of her weeping speak to my skin through the flimsy double layer of our summer clothing; nor had I ears, throughout the journey, for anything but those intermittent sobs. Alvise said nothing; I watched the electricity poles coming up and ripping past, as if we were competing in our own private "Targa Florio", as that race was driven once upon a time, by night, by the light of the Milky Way alone, on the dirt roads and bone-shaking cart tracks of pre-War days. Every bump, and there were plenty of them, threw her bodice upon my heart, muslin against alpaca; and the soft tears falling, the cyclamens of her breath. . . So I couldn't help but stroke her hair, gently, as one strokes a venerable family cat; and then her whole face, as well as I could make it out in the dark, or conjure it up from memory: the broad, white forehead above a pair of artful, enigmatic eyes, with a look of stubbornness and self-reliance, as of someone with but one thought in mind and no wish to share it. And then that nose, so treacherously chiselled, and the lips that seemed to make love to one another . . . It made me feel (must I confess it?) a languor, a perturbation . . . Gesualdo! What on earth has come over you?

Alvise turned round from time to time, but in that darkness it was a pure formality. In any case, after all the pandemonium, he had subsided, except for the same old sarcastic chuckle which occasionally sprouted anew in the dark interior of the car. If anything it was Iaccarino who had grown vigilant and grim: a Great Dane on guard, a sentry on watch at an arsenal. The back of his neck seemed alarmed, preoccupied, aware of my tremblings in the back seat. He trod all the harder on the accelerator in order to get home before dawn if possible, as the old man wanted. Nothing doing. All too soon day was already breaking, and we would inevitably be forced to expose ourselves to the cheeky scrutiny of the milkman, and to the lynx-eyed curiosity of Donna Rosa Pitoncia, as she washed down the piece of pavement at her door.

I didn't care, I watched the dawn; how long since I'd watched it last! Clasping Maria Venera round the waist, as she slept like a girl-child on my chest, I nuzzled my nose though her hair and turned to the rear window to see, after the first small skirmishes of the light, the birth and growth in the east of an immense butterfly-wing. By this time we were speeding between the first houses, which still retained the night; but behind us, and from the perfect angle, the sun was lighting a splendid early Monet, a radiant plain on a summer's morning, and that vast butterfly outspread above it, from tip to tip of the horizon; pools of water shining in it like eyes; between the sea and the vineyards a winding gleam of asphalt, which in that light seemed to take on the graces of a river. Everywhere pine and cypress, hillock and hollow, cerulean stumps of ancient stone . . . To the left, the green bay of Punta Scalambra. Another minute and I'd have wept.

FIRST ASIDE

The author's first doubts concerning the book he is writing.

Whoa there! Where am I going? The fable is getting out of hand, memory is clowning it behind my back. The same thing with the words: they're coming out cockeyed, scoffing, souped-up bittersweetmeats hellbent on corruption, the corruption of a boy, of a teenage memory within me . . . Great stuff, now that I'm old, to poke fun at the boy I was; to cash in, like some crafty rain-king, on the weather forecast I heard just now on the radio. Great stuff . . . I now know all about myself: where the roundabout routes of fate were heading me, the infatuated urgings of the blood. But why unload today's pretensions on yesterday's apprentice? On the other hand, what can a trapped mouse *do*? Just eat the bait, was the advice given me by a gentleman on the train between Sapri and Salerno in September '81. And so?

So, dear reader, allow me to go on as I am, trundling my body ahead at random, this juke-box of memories programmed to disobey. And expect from me nothing resembling the kind of reading you have enjoyed to date. No serenading fiddlesticks or braying trumpets, Tusitalan telling of tales or mirror in Main Street, Alice's looking glass or through-a-glass-darkly; no opium-eaters, lotus-eaters, annunciating angels; no patience played on St Helena or light sibylline leaf at Cumae . . . No, but the secret of an ass-eared king whispered to the reeds in a ditch, a Moral Operetta with music by Offenbach, a Dialogue of a Physicist and a Metaphysician refereed by a Pataphysician . . . A fraud, in fact, a trifling drollery, to set a screen between me and that old temptation, to purge my thoughts of utterblack, utterblank, utternothing; to deter me from the effort of slashing my wrists, half-heartedly, every four months . . . Or call it a dramatization, call it what you will, as long as it serves instead of life for me. Peg-leg literature, how does that strike you? Pirated of course . . . And not just to make the alliteration more appetizing, but because I really need it: a surrogate for life by day and a surrogate for sleep, when I cannot sleep, by night. As you know, it takes a mere nothing to prevent me from sleeping at night. Whereas, if I get into the habit of counting, not sheep, but people . . . characters; if, to every rule of metrics and rhetoric that acts like a policeman on point-duty I succeed in delivering myself up, a blissful slave, then who knows what might not . . .

Shall I proceed, then? I proceed.

FOUR

The author's love of armchair adventure. Impromptu by Iaccarino philosopher, and report on the first visit to Venera.

For the part it has played in my life, I have always credited adventure and its attendant emotions with the virtues of invigorating gymnastics. How vastly more healthy is a racing heart than an aching heart or a breaking heart! I recall that as a boy, on thieving escapades to the vineyards, I would choose nights of full moon and the vines closest to the sleeping night-watchman. And what a fright, and what delight, as my lips pulled at the full, dark, breast-like bunches.

In later days I loved dubious alleyways, raffish companions, tales of cloak and dagger. I was given to perusing the old newspaper serials in the attic, eager to catch the warning signal of the hurdy-gurdy lookout-man posted at the corner. I would dearly have liked to experience a *mystère de Paris* in flesh and blood, to play Russian roulette just the once, to receive a letter from the Black Hand, signed with a cross. I am still attracted by the least thing containing a risk. Even in my taste for daydreaming, my theatre of shut-your-eyes-and-enter, I rejoice every time I can twist things into some imagined hazard. As if, stock still, I aimed to imitate a sleepwalker pacing a sill six inches wide, and in my thought repeat his deadly anaesthesias . . .

This explains why, in all the unforeseen events of that night, even the commonplace ones, I strove to catch at the slightest hint of adventurous extravaganza; and even now as I write I relish it all over again with a sort of sedentary fervour, if I may so call the blend of passion and distance which my dreams are made on. Add to this the pleasure of strolling about in a plot that is rather, if not royally, cooked up; in a depravity and irony of words; in an etching barely corroded by the acid of the possible; the pleasure, that is, of playing puppet and puppeteer at once in one of the countless puppet-shows of this loathsome-lovesome life . . .

I got to school late that day. Reaching home at dawn, I slept like the dead for a while, head on the kitchen table amidst a congeries of empty carafes and bottles that might have been a bad copy of a twentieth-century Bolognese Master. Madama's double black coffee failed to put me to rights, so I entered the classroom at the speed of a hearse, albeit with that intellectual air which weariness bestows on even the most insipid features.

It was one of the last classes of the year, and the exams were pressing close upon us, so I expected the girls to keep quiet and pay some attention. But on the contrary, all I got were little grins and giggles. At first I didn't catch on. It took me a while to absorb the fact that they were looking at me in a special way, as if they saw me walking on a cloud, or hovering kite-like above their heads. Then it dawned on me that they were proud of me, proud of sharing the secret of an *affaire de coeur*. The truth was, the news of that awful night, and the part I had played in bringing back the lamb to the fold, had spread like wildfire and, magnified by fictional acts of valour, had reached the bars where the girls habitually stopped to eat a bun, the stationer's where they had bought a pen-nib. So they cast me furtive, gratified, conspiratorial looks, and were suddenly, sweetly subservient. Such power over those unguarded imaginations had the aroma of scandal raining upon them from the podium, that it instantly dispelled any solidarity with the fugitive, and raised me to the rank of paladin on the field. For my part, with those black rings under my eyes, that intrepid plaster stuck on my temple, right on the knock-out spot, with a shirt all crumpled and still redolent of her, I felt set free from all past diffidence, a St George no less invincible than the St George at Ibla, carved in stone above a portal, skewering the dragon on his long lance.

I felt obliged, despite my good mood, to torment a certain Esther Catafalmo, and a certain Lucia Vacirca, both of the back bench, by replacing the *Paradiso* they were sharing, dense with pencilled cribs, with my own little red Dante with not a note in it. Out of magnanimity I did not mark them down, but dismissed them with the air of a king signing a pardon, winding up with a harangue on the duties of youth, the which however, I don't know how, became a "Gather ye rosebuds while ye may", and was an unparalleled success. Acquitted in advance by the wisecrack with which I rounded this off, "So don't miss the buss, miss!" they raised the roof: I had them in the palm of my hand.

Quite another story with the headmaster, Biscari, when he sent for the pair of us, me and Iaccarino. Nothing to reproach us for, of course; we had helped in a sacred cause, averted a dastardly deed. Nevertheless, one had to think of the good name of the school. It is not right for the physicians of souls to mix in worldly matters. Even with the best intentions. Even without sullying one's hands. Another time, therefore, please think twice.

We didn't answer back. The headmaster was a fair-minded man, heavy on Maths and light on Letters, as ingenuous as a Hail Mary. Liable to biliousness, with a complexion as yellow as a Chinese flied plawn vendor, he was not a person to drive up the pole. Nor, to be honest, did he deserve the frauds perpetrated on him by Iaccarino, who found it too good to be true, to be able with perfect impunity to inundate him with spurious quotations and authorities. As he now did, turning the conversation onto Galfo and (Alvise *dixerat*) his supposed shortcomings.

"He is lacking something," he commented, while Biscari nodded in some perplexity, "and it is a very important lacuna. The same which is discussed with Abelard by Sister Mariana Alcoforado in the *Sonnets from the Portuguese*."

I pretended to yawn, to cover up my laughter, and things went from bad to worse.

"*Errando discitur*," observed Iaccarino, and paraphrased at once: "We live and yawn," eliciting a timorous squeak of protest from the headmaster.

On this note we left, but I sensed that, now his high spirits had simmered down, Iaccarino was not happy. More and more often these days he would butterfly about with words, only to go all glum a moment later. To distract him I asked him about the damage to the car, and offered to pay for it in instalments, but he didn't seem to grasp what I was saying, burrowing deeper down into his meagre, bachelor bones.

"There's this feeling," he said at last, "this feeling that's making my heart ache. When I do some everyday thing, like smoke a cigarette, say hullo, listen to a song, it occurs to me that, who knows, maybe it's the last time I'll smoke, or listen, or say hullo, and that we're all dying; and that to die is just as inchoative a verb as to live . . ."

He was silent for a moment, lit a cigarette, and threw it away after the first puff.

"I'm getting old, my friend, don't you see?" he burst out. "Where is the Pietro of yesteryear, the Duke of Norfolk's pretty page-boy? I've lost a night's sleep and I'm feeling it; I've ruined a fine abduction and I'm sorry. Believe me, they're slandering Liborio. He and Venera, he's a dolt and she's a dolt, and believe me they would have been happy. No, don't say no. You're just as silly as they are."

He raised his eyes to the heavens.

"I believe in order," he said, "and your love is a disorder. That is, a mere will-o'-the-wisp. Because every disorder on earth is a deception, dust thrown in our eyes to flummox us. That conjuror fellow, God the Father, you see, is not only clever, but cheats. However, Pietrino here is not taken in, Pietrino has a discriminating nose. He can smell out His spoor in the sand even if He does cover his tracks by putting His shoes on back to front . . ."

He blew his nose loudly. "Everything is order," he cried.

"There is in nature no kink or cacophony which cannot be made to toe the line by means of alphabets, Richter scales, *Grandes Larousses*. Even my nose, look – this cabbage-stalk, this flaming haemorrhoid – well it's not this sort of nose by chance, it's not just the misspelling of a drunken scrivener. It's a caption to my character, an eruptive exemplification of myself: exactly what is needed to undeceive the myopic, the monoculous, the crosseyed, the blind . . ."

"Yes, but what's that got to do with me?" I was really narked.

"Because you're a dolt," he replied somewhat illogically, "a juggins and in love, a muddle among the countless ostentatious, phoney muddles in the cosmos, which I refuse to approve. You are all of you clouds, you lovers, clouds that dishevel the sky. Do you see those two clouds resting on the top of Monserrato, white, frothy and silly? Now do you see that third one, all dark and doltish, annoying them, hovering and yapping and playing the cur in front of them? The top two are Liborio and Venera, the one below is you: a wisp of silly cotton-wool – one puff of wind and you'd be blown to shreds . . ."

I did my best to put up with this, but the joke turned sour and irritating: "To be silly, friend, is one of the most widely publicized rights of man. It is mentioned in the Law of the Twelve Tables . . ."

He didn't let me finish: "You're a babe in arms, that's what you are. All winter you've been traipsing after her to no avail, while all that bloke needed was a moustache and a pair of nimble feet . . ."

I turned on my heel, but he dashed after me, full of concern. "Don't mind me," he said. "I say things because I'm fond of you, and sometimes I say too much. But I saw you being so mawkish in the car, and the girl seems such a flibberty-gibbet that I expect no good to come of this frenzy of yours. It was better before, when you kept your trap shut and wrote her poems. Anyway, what are you hoping for? What do you want?"

I squeezed his arm, surprised and grateful. I was pleased that after all that carry-on about chaos and order my friend deigned to say a few kind words, and take a humble interest for a while in me. Even if fleetingly, it was some compensation for the intimacies I'd missed in adolescence, those mournful confidences between chums walking endlessly from one front door to the other and back, always meaning to say goodbye but never doing it. In any case, if he hadn't been so human a buffoon, this Iaccarino, would I have been so fond of him?

"I love her in a different way now," I claimed. "Now she and I have a memory to share."

"A disgrace, you mean. She won't forgive you for catching her like that."

"On the contrary," I maintained. "Lots of love-affairs spring from sharing a disgraceful secret."

He pulled a face. "You just see if she doesn't go off with the other chap again."

"Not likely, now that she's seen him in his socks and his hitch-me-ups."

I took his arm, and we strolled down the Corso under the arcades. It was nearly two in the afternoon, and the town seemed uninhabited. Everyone was having lunch or taking a nap; the sun seemed to just hang there, going neither forwards nor backwards.

How warm and good it is, I thought, this minute of youth. How I want to sip at it, slowly. How warm and good is life.

On Sunday afternoon I climbed up to Alvise's palazzo, tracked down on his behalf by a lad called Vincenzo, a Moorish-faced foundling who in the days of prosperity had been in the old man's service, and now eked out a living as a footslogging courier between the two Módicas, in competition with the costly taxis. Vincenzo was his name, but with the addition of at least three nicknames: *Zichitiniellu*, whatever that may mean; *Scappaleggbia*, or Lightshoe; and finally, more learnedly, at the suggestion of us teachers, Puck; due partly to the elfin curls around the quaintest, most mischievous face you can imagine, and partly to his nature, which led him to appear, to disappear, to weave plots, to mix up messages . . . Each time uttering a trill of laughter which seemed forced but wasn't: it genuinely sprang from the delight of being able to dispel all fear of retribution by the simple emission of a crystalline gurgle.

Vincenzo now came to tell me that they were expecting me at the palazzo, and darted away with the tip in his hand, while I stood wavering at the corner of the old Passo Carrafa, which was the way up.

It took a whale of breath and knee-work to reach the big palazzo, to which clung scarcely a ghost of the old stucco, beneath cornices of soft stone almost totally eaten away by the years. Calcabrina, Barbariccia, Alichino did not deem me worthy of a nod as I looked up at them, nor could I have sworn whether the whisk of a hem glimpsed at a window above belonged to a garment or to a snatch of net curtain. Certainly, there was no need to knock, as the great door creaked open on its own.

On the landing at the top of the twenty-seven steps I was met not by the maid Anita, but by Alvise in person, emaciated, with the skin over his jaw as waxy and tight as onion-skin: a helpless shinbone-of-a-saint all ready for promotion to the reliquary. Quite another matter from the Knight Templar armed with a mace and a flower in his buttonhole who until yesterday harangued us on the pavement. I didn't stop to wonder whether it was distress at what had happened or the lack of his dentures that had brought him so low; I was convinced it was the contagion of the house, that skeleton of a house, which made its inmates and owners like unto itself. To such an extent that I feared at any moment Venera herself might appear in the doorway as a skull, or some other fleshless, flat-nosed effigy.

Not a bit of it. Venera gave me the lie at once, and her skull, so to speak, displayed cheeks and lips more engaging than ever, burgeoning like a rosy bloom from her white frilly collar.

It was the first chance I'd had of taking a good, long look at her. At other times, at the dance, at the concert, during the red-handed episode at the hotel and the return journey in the car, there had always been some impediment, too much light or too little, some haste or paralysis of the heart, to upset my contemplation of her. I had never before been in the position of spectator and judge, always in the less tranquil one of snooper, if not indeed of the accused. But this time things were different. This interview had been requested, the debit was on her side, whereas I had a right to the privileges of a creditor. I therefore looked at her as if from the front row of the stalls, inch by inch, from the tresses gathered at the nape of her neck into a great fist of a chignon, the olive forehead, the high cheekbones, to the nervous twitching of her nostrils. *Boookarooo* went her voice in the glades of her throat, *boookarooo*, *bookarooo*.

However, it was Alvise who spoke first, while his granddaughter gave occasional nods of assent, though it was not clear whether her behaviour expressed her true sentiments, or was the effect of the medicines they had bucked her up with. Be that as it may, it was a new Venera, at once resolute and docile, who assented to what Alvise said, dissembling beneath the pallors of dishonoured womanhood the martial scowl of Judith in arms, to whom above all others I saw fit to liken her. A new Venera, the soul of good sense. Although from time to time two irascible pupils pawed the ground beneath her brows and the ice of her forehead crackled.

The old man's voice was subdued, and as he spoke his fingers twisted away at the pon-pon of the cap he had just taken off. He was not concerned about the talk around town, he said. He cared only about a few, the esteem of a few . . . He gave me a meaning glance, forcing from me a whispered "Thank you" that only Venera heard. Yes, it had been a headstrong act, a children's outing, he said. But only one thing mattered: the girl had not been molested.

I avoided her eyes, concentrating fiercely on a glass bell-jar, the kind of thing which in the South in the old days used to stand on the chest-of-drawers and contain a wax figure of the Infant Jesus. This one, to be frank, encased a more frivolous trophy: a pair of silken hose wound round a pair of dainty black leather shoes.

Alvise followed my eyes, emitted his usual sardonic laugh, and said "A souvenir," while Venera flushed scarlet: "You know, that Baden-Baden business. It was in all the papers fifty years ago."

I pretended to follow him, though I was astonished by the inconsistency I seemed to detect in his behaviour. The more he posed, regarding his past, as a rake on a European scale, the more, regarding his grand-daughter, he demoted himself to the level of a conscientious, indigenous guardian, informing me that it was his intention to have her resume her interrupted studies – not at the *Conservatoire*, which no longer mattered, but the more modest, easily-achieved schoolwork, though with private lessons. Three months of study would perhaps suffice to gain her diploma in the autumn exams, and the hope of a job, *lejos, muy lejos de aquí*. Therefore if I, with a few lessons, remunerated, needless to say . . .

I accepted effusively, declining, as he expected, the idea of recompense, and in return received thanks and courtesies, while Maria Venera said nothing, but looked on with contrite brow. She was sitting opposite me, but might have been kneeling in prayer, such was the penitence of the gaze which from her low chair rose towards me.

"You can start tomorrow," said Don Alvise. "Make arrangements between yourselves; I'm already late for my nap." And giving me an unexpected wink, the only sign of life in a face like a shoehorn, with shuffling steps he went upon his way.

FIVE

Duet with Venera. The postman always takes the knocks. Revelations concerning the House of Trubia. With Venera again: "*parthenía, parthenía . . .*"

Alone with Maria Venera. A little table between us, with books on it, a white notepad, a pot of green ink. A little table, a long distance. Not unlike the distance duellists pace out before they turn . . . Though our behaviour is not that of combat, but of etiquette: neither will fire first.

My voice sounds strange to me, as always when I'm with a woman. She has the air of an unctuous hypocrite, a hostess untrustworthy or treacherous.

"Would you care for a walnut liqueur? Home-made, you know."

Liqueur? Never again! Not with these flames roaring up and down my cheeks. I didn't even know how to address her, formally or familiarly. She plumped for the familiar.

Alone with Maria Venera, my brand-new pupil, so demure and goody-goody, discoursing so primly about the syllabus, the textbooks she had and didn't have . . . As time was short, wouldn't an abridgement do? And as for the Greek classic . . . and *fòl dol de di do*.

"I can make it by October," she concluded in a rush, as if she were entrusting my ear with an admission of guilt or the password of a conspiracy.

I simply don't understand. Can this be the insurgent girl who so lately, in the arms of the dancing-man, was on the brink of the crucial *paso doble* of her life? And why, over everything she says, does she smarm the unctuousness of a sly caress? It leaves me baffled. Still fresh in my memory, ingrowing like a toenail, is the sight of the two of them in the hotel, and I can't bring myself to believe in such a lightning change of heart. They are slandering Galfo, according to Iaccarino. A trifle effeminate, perhaps, but how many are – and then go fathering young like rabbits. Anyway, down here in the South, any pretty boy who doesn't flaunt Virility with a capital V arouses suspicions of that sort, to which life almost always seems to give the lie. But as for Venera, well, she chose him after all, so how come she seems to have forgotten all about him, discoursing about syllabuses and exam questions as cool as you please, poker faced, with not a tremor, not a sign of remorse . . .

Such, for me, was this bed of thorns, that I couldn't resist hounding her: "Well then, have you nothing to tell me?"

She was silent, stared at the floor, and nervously slipped a ring on and off her finger.

"I can help you. I'm . . . very fond of you."

I stumbled over the words, yammered them between my teeth, trying to smuggle in the declaration of love as a harmless statement of brotherly good will. But she bowled me over by doing three things in quick succession: she burst into tears, tears as large as hailstones; she hurled herself blindly against me, head down as if to dash her brains out, and hunted for my mouth with open lips; finally, after a brief, moist touch of tongues, she slipped from my grasp, gagged my mouth with one hand, and with the other slapped herself savagely on the right cheek. "Poor me, poor me!" she moaned, as she returned to the clinch, the scent of her drenching me, arching her back to foil me, however, as soon as I tried to return her fervour, and at the same time smiling at me between bouts of tears. Those tears, that impetuosity restrained, but not so far as to appear rejection, left me flabbergasted. Could it just be a trick to disarm me, make me a partner to her plans? Or was it not, rather, intrinsic to the cat in her to steep every gesture of limb or of heart in such oils of innocent wantonness? This was the misgiving that milled within me, and she sensed it as if I had shouted it aloud.

"Tomorrow I'll explain everything," she said, pulling herself together and obliging me to return to my role as tutor. Not a moment too soon, for in the door opposite I had seen the handle slowly turning . . .

"Manzoni," I therefore craftily declaimed, "in his *Letter to M. Chauvet* . . ." And here was Alvise entering the room in time for the syllables of that foreign name to kindle a liquid light behind his eyelids, resurrecting before him, as in a fortune-teller's crystal mirror, memories of distant waters and of spas, of parasols, gardens, veiled faces, *aigrettes*, vows of eternal love exchanged behind a fan . . .

"Show-vay, did you say? In 'Twenty-One, no, in 'Twenty-Two, I . . ."

When I explained that it must be a simple case of homonymy, he looked at me with a touch of resentment, breaking off the story he was embarking on. So I did not learn then, and very likely would never learn, who she was, and what he had shared, while taking the waters together at Vichy, that June of 'Twenty-Two, or 'Twenty-One, with a certain Mlle. Marie-Edwige Chauvet . . .

When I left, Venera saw me to the door. "The address is on it," she whispered, slipping a wax-sealed envelope into my pocket without giving me time to ask what sort of mission she intended to entrust me with. The duel lasted almost no time at all, between the alarm-bell that started shrilling in one ear and the pealing alleluias triumphant in the other. It needed no more, as we said goodbye, than the pressure of her hand in mine, and the alleluias ran riot in me, kept me glorious company as I all but sprinted from San Giovanni to Lower Módica, down, down, down the old serpent of stone steps.

As soon as I reached "The Salon", lit like day by a double row of dazzling globes, and my elation was beginning to wane, I was cut to the quick by the address I made out on the package. I was expecting Liborio Galfo and I found Rosario Trubia. Trubia, no less! Maria Venera's cousin, the womanizer Sasà Trubia! Ah then this little gift began to burn my fingers. It was not, woe alas, as I had hoped, returning the abductor's letters, but rather . . . but rather, what? Had I not been the gentleman I was, I would have rushed off and artfully explored the package, as if taking a sample from a water-melon, or a miner's core-specimen, or making the biopsy of a suspected tumour . . . As it was I stood torturing myself, unable to make up my mind either to crack it or to post it.

"With Grandpa Alvise, mum's the word," she had urged me on the doorstep, squeezing my hand hard. Yet another reason to think that the prisoner must set great store by this postman business, seeing that she dared not use the services of the lad *Zichitiniellu*, but prefered a grown-up booby, a lovelorn stooge. And furthermore, when I considered the fact that in Sicily the first never-to-be-forgotten love of every girl-cousin is her boy-cousin . . . Enough! Everything led to the supposition that my rivals were two in number, and the second a far greater threat than the first.

This Sasà Trubia, I knew him well. He was one of Venera's many cousins, all male, all called Trubia, all sons of Aunts Severa and Prudenzia, who took the girl with them on their holidays every summer. Rich and ugly, they had been married on the same day (it turned out to be the day of the Treaty of Versailles) to the two wealthy, draft-dodging Trubia brothers, leaving their younger sister Grazia to fall for and pursue a legionnaire from Fiume. The latter, before he died, collaborated with zest in begetting Maria Venera, and with still greater zest in squandering all her hopes of a dowry, present or future, in partnership with Don Alvise. Concerning father-in-law and son-in-law there persisted in Módica (after all those years I was still in time to catch its afterglow) a legend of transalpine sprees, baggageless flits, compulsory repatriations, following a more or less seasonal timetable, punctuated by the forlorn picture of Donna Grazia seated on a bench in the waiting room of some loan-shark, or some smart aleck of a magistrate. So that's the way the money went, and that's the way she went as well, gentle little *garçonne* of a Grazia, with her bobbed hair, gazing at me out of a cheap frame on Maria Venera's table.

Things had been different for Severa and Prudenzia: ample progeny, good health, affluence. Their two Trubia husbands had long been industrious ants in the cement business, building roads, schools, rural dwellings. Not without the help of the local Fascist juntas, whose zealous supporters they professed to be, as of other more occult eminences up in Rome, where they made a pilgrimage every New Year's Day, taking with them the "oilcan", or the "roly-poly" as they called it. This was a bulging concertina-briefcase, excellent for lubricating every lubricable wheel. Now that one of the brothers was dead, and the other off his rocker, the widow and the semi-widow, in spite of having been christened prudent and severe, had taken to making injudicious speculations and spending money madly. To the point of keeping open house up at La Sorda every summer, in the hope, it was said, of finding advantageous matches for their bachelor sons; who in truth showed no haste in the matter, but were more inclined to lend a hand in dissipating the last of the family possessions.

Sasà was the least handsome of the four cousins, but the most predatory, with that wiry black beard on his jawbone, that haughty, rampant nose, and the eyes of a heraldic beast. With a touch of eccentricity to boot, seeing as he would make frequent trips on a Vespa up the lanes of Ammazzanuvole, dressed as an artist in floppy velvet beret and flowing cravat, presenting to the mooing amazement of the cattle out to grass the spectacle of an easel slung over his shoulder and, in his saddlebag, a paintbox that was a perfect rainbow. Probably all an act, since no one ever saw a finished canvas, while malignant tongues spoke of trysts with the daughter of a goldsmith who had a house in those parts . . .

Now I was good friends with this lad, because we were both

jazz fiends, lending each other records every day and exchanging enthusiasms. I was not pleased, therefore, to find in him an elusive adversary, scarcely visible behind the screen of Galfo; and moreover with the prospect of myself playing the part of an amatory Mercury. The packet in my hand grew leaden, and I couldn't stop prodding it, sniffing it, wondering what ethereal auras, as often happens with objects, impregnated it with thought and passion, and whether I might be able to interpret them. My great dread, needless to say, was that it contained love-tokens, fresh collusions behind the backs of Alvise and myself on the part of the prisoner (for Maria Venera was indeed such, sealed up in the house with seven seals, waiting for the scandal to die down). I felt excluded, humiliated that she didn't scruple to make use of me, with insolent indifference and not a thought for my feelings, to send a message saying goodness knows what to a probable gallant. And finally, if this was so, what the devil was the meaning of her elopement with Galfo? A sense of dudgeon, such as every mystery arouses in me, began to gnaw at my heart; and the voice within me which day and night repeated "Venera, I love you," was joined by another: "Venera, to a nunnery go, farewell!"

In this predicament, Licausi did less than nothing to help. I came across him drooping about outside the chemist's shop run by the Fratantonios, husband and wife, pretending with one eye to read the cinema posters, and with the other, more sharply focused, exploring the gaps between the jars displayed in the window, endeavouring to catch a glimpse within of the lovely face of their daughter, Isolina. Feeling in no mood to compete with his contemplations, I preferred to take my disgruntlement for a walk, until at last I resolved to thrust the envelope, with furtive fingers, into the letter-box at the corner of the Town Hall.

When I reached home, and had disengaged myself from the attentions of Madama Amalia, and shut my door behind me, there, on the usual paper blackboard pinned to the wall, giving me three ironical cheers, was my latest hymn in praise of Venera. TO MARIA VENERA was the title written in large block letters at the top. And I, in an impulsive act of faith, filling the only blank space on the sheet of paper, added TO MARIA VERGINE in equally big letters below, as when two peasants at the notary's align their signatures one beneath the other at the foot of an Agreement.

Immediately afterwards, sleep carried me off.

That vote of confidence I was forced to revoke with a stroke of the pen twenty-four hours later, following a second meeting with the girl over an anthology of early Italian poetry which, as a good omen for seduction, I had opened at the page devoted to Cielo d'Alcamo.

"I'm expecting a baby," she began point-blank. Then, all in one breath, "It's not Galfo's, it's someone else's, someone who doesn't want me, and doesn't know about it, and who I don't want any more, and if he did know he'd marry me, but I wouldn't marry him."

"Oh my God!" I babbled in the best tradition of Mariccia's favourite reading. And it flashed into my mind how deeply moved would be our dear Amapola, had she been listening from behind the threadbare brocade curtain. I babbled, but my distress was mingled with a curious sense of satisfaction. Not only because a single certainty seemed to me better than a thousand doubts, but because I myself would have a part, even though a mere supporting role, to play in such an exuberantly comic plot. So true it was, and I say it now with an old man's hindsight, that at that time I needed the footlights of love far more than the fact of it.

"What's Galfo got to say about it?" I asked, obediently accepting the office of confidant.

"Galfo knows everything, he was the only one to know, and he immediately suggested running away and getting married." A slight flush came to her cheeks. "He was perfectly happy to take responsibility for this child, that isn't his. Mostly out of kindness to me, but also, I think, to get his own back and give the lie to some of the things they say about him."

"Are they true?"

The question slipped out, fatuous as it was, and I was instantly ashamed of it. But she shrugged.

"It doesn't matter if they're true. Better, in fact." Then, when her face had lost its flush and its flurry, with a touch of bravado which lent her voice a resolute edge, she added, "He's a kind soul, Galfo, and I'm fond of him. Apart from that, I needed a father for this one" – she thumped her belly with her fist – "and a husband for myself, so that coming out of Mass together we could walk arm in arm under his balcony . . ." She stopped her mouth with the back of her hand, but the bird had flown: it wasn't hard to guess which balcony she meant, for opposite the church there was only that of her relatives the Trubias.

That pantomime of reticence made me smile, though. As if the name on the package hadn't already been clear proof . . . And after all, if she disclosed the fact to me, why all the secrecy about the culprit? But Maria Venera was made that way, as I was to realize later on closer acquaintance: a hotch-potch of brazenness and blushes, superfluous lies and impulsive confessions, calculations measured by the ticking of a time-bomb and impetuous recklessness in word and deed. A babel of a girl, in whom a hundred languages gave tongue simultaneously, one proceeding from her irrepressible sensuality, another from her passionate, covetous mind, another from vanity, another from pride, yet another from fear . . .

I now know, for it is common knowledge in these parts, that in the place where she now lives, *lejos, muy lejos de aquí*, she has devoted herself to good works, and if she listens to a voice it is that of heaven. But, in those days, with what douceur did she belong to the devil! With what bonds of vulpine and columbine guile was she bound to him!

To be acquitted, though. To be acquitted whatever she said or did. For that gift of inordinate beauty that she shed upon the world, and her defencelessness of heart, her way of yielding herself willingly and lovingly to the light. Acquitted like me, like everyone else. For whom, on the face of the earth, would I not acquit, what Cain or what Judas, since all are so wretched, so helpless, so loving of their light-encompassed selves, suspended so, and close to falling (in a year, in a minute) from their patch of light into the darkness! Dying indeed, having to die, redeems every trespass; nor is there anyone living, even the most innocent, who will in the end be reprieved from sentence of death.

I therefore acquitted Maria Venera; in fact, I dangled a carrot.

"You can still marry Galfo if you want to."

She gave me a disconsolate look: "I can't any more, I don't want to any more. I was already sorry after half an hour in the car, and I only went on with it to be fair to him. Now I want to be rid of this baby and everyone else as well. I've given the other his marching orders by letter. As for Liborio, *you're* going to tell him."

She assumed such a gladiatorial air that I dared not breathe a word. Though I would have liked to tell her I didn't believe her, that she was still mad about Trubia.

But now the dam had burst.

"Get rid of it, kill it; this seed that's been planted inside me! It'll be like killing the father."

"What a thing to say!" I protested mildly. "And anyway, how will you manage it?"

"I can raise the money by selling mother's old jewellery. For everything else I'm counting on your help, because you've got a good heart. I know of a woman who does these things. I only have to get to Catania, to an address I know . . ."

She lowered her eyes to the text before us, and they happened to light on the line, "You can do this deed sooner than crack an egg." At which she burst into such a tremendous peal of laughter that it must have frightened Alvise down below in his study, where he was, I imagine, engrossed in browsing through his bound copies of *Paris s'amuse, Ludovic Baschet, éditeur*.

He knocked, he poked his head in: "What's up?"

"Nothing," I replied. "It's just that one of these days I'm going to have to nip up to Catania, and after all this time indoors Venera would like to come with me and do some window-shopping. May we?"

SIX

Spying from a high window. Letter to Angel Archangel. Galfo as his own second. Disquisition on anonymous letters.

"At the dawn of Nothingness
There was a light, and consciousness,
A palimpsest, a kind
Of mishmash in the mind,
Creation being created
By a process unabated . . ."

I was on my bed racking my brains for a sequel when Madama intoned,

"Mimosa, mimosa,
Oh, the sadness of your smile . . ."

in a throaty voice, combing her hair the while, and eyeing her reflection in the chancy mirror of my window-panes. A habit I had declared war on from the first, but which enabled her at one and the same time to gratify two quite different duties and pleasures: matutinal care of her person and curiosity about the affairs of her neighbours, as viewed through a natural peephole between two pots of parsley. Her target was the building opposite, a many-windowed apartment-house where they put on a free show, not only at dawn, but twenty-four hours out of twenty-four. From my belvedere one could follow the most private and variegated manifestations of living, quarrels and truces, scrimpings and squanderings. One could count the items and changes of underwear, spy out a thousand and one choice secrets, the arrivals and departures of tradesmen, of debtors, of creditors, the progress of a death or the budding of a puberty. Must I confess that, some mornings, when Amalia invaded my quarters with the excuse of coming to wake me, even I allowed myself to be drawn into becoming her accomplice in espionage? To gather material for the books I would some day write, I maintained; although I could hardly include in this pretext the attention I paid to the lacy impalpables and black silk furbelows hung out on the balcony of the young girl Isolina. No sooner out of bed but this girl, in dressing-gown and slippers, started walloping a carpet with a carpet beater, and with this racket insinuated herself into my drowsy awakening. Once on my feet, I set my hand to a naval telescope, extorted from Madama's jealous grasp, and shadowed the girl from room to room, watched her come and go from bathroom to breakfast, her movements loitering and listless; watched her coolly make coffee, coolly peel some fruit, smoke a cigarette, give a yawn. Finally, at eight twenty-eight precisely, *voilà*, there she is all ready, goodness knows how, with her school overalls clinging to limbs as nimble as a goat's, dashing headlong out and flashing around the corner of the Narrows, where the "Salon" begins to soar upwards.

Isolina was studying to be a teacher at the school where I taught, but in a different section. Licausi, who had a weakness for schoolgirls, had little by little been taken with her as a result of encounters in the corridor, confining himself to date, in order to see her again in the afternoon, to going more often than necessary to her parents' pharmacy, where he was only too pleased to wait around prevaricating and letting other people get served first, until finally he was obliged to buy at least a packet of bicarbonate of soda, usually without having caught a glimpse of the girl. He made no fuss about this, his affections as yet being only lukewarm. For Licausi was, or seemed, a lukewarm, cautious type in whose heart feelings arrived on tiptoe and took months and months to come to a head.

For my part, I had for quite some time had my eye on this Isolina-across-the-way. I had even smiled at her, that Sunday when Madama's cat, Quo Vadis? by name, had got trapped, amid loud lamentations, in a very narrow gutter, and the neighbours were out watching from their terraces and balconies. Unable to turn round, Quo Vadis? had long hesitated, huffing and puffing over the abyss; then he had made the spirited decision to jump for it, and plummeted down like an anvil into the ocean. Only to get to his feet at once without a scratch on him, shake a little dust from his fur, and stroll homewards as placid as you please. It was then that I smiled at her, while holding the animal up by the scruff of the neck and presenting him to the plaudits of the audience. And she smiled back.

Madama, questioned, informed me that *Mimosa* was a song from thirty years back, and that her father had sung it to her when she was still a little girl. Little girl? I couldn't help laughing. I entertained too many speculations about her age to give her the benefit of *that* calculation. On the other hand, in view of the use I made of it, her florid maturity was no bad thing. Foolhardy to have delegated the task of cooling my young blood to less ripe charms. In carnal matters, in those days, I was both easy-going and fastidious. On the rare occasions when my friends dragged me by force to some suburban brothel, if I made a choice at all she was bound to be the dowdiest, the most time-worn and buffeted, fearful as I was that any of the others would somehow cramp my style. I declined even the alluring assistant madam, Zoë, excluded from consumption by *hoi polloi* but always available to the more refined clientele. Not for me. The splendours of Zoë, though somewhat crumpled by professional use, never failed to overawe me, and I therefore contented myself with the vagrant whores who were moved on every fortnight. Save for falling back in the end, my bolt-hole, my bulwark, my bethel, on the hallowed bridal chamber of Madama. The same who now, without ceasing to apostrophize Mimosa at the top of her voice, brandished a hair-clogged comb at the street below to point out the invariable morning changing of the guard between a husband in working boots on his way out and ex-M.P. Scillieri, the Man in the Street, on his way in . . .

I didn't waste much time chortling over this. I was in a hurry. Another day awaited me, as full as an egg: the last class at school, the visit to Maria Venera to arrange what to do about her emergency; not to mention, in the interval, lunch at Don Cesare's with the predictable interpolations from the opposition benches . . . So I rushed off. But at the classroom door Ermenegilda handed me not only the class register but a perfumed letter, delivered with the morning post.

I love getting letters. I am seized by a modest transport whenever I can sink into an armchair with a rug over my knees, a paper-knife in hand, beside a pile of beautiful, bellying envelopes. As lovely, indeed, before being emptied of their contents, as afterwards they are ragged and repulsive, when they stand revealed, practically always, as impudent tax demands, circulars from the tenants' committee, links in some nitwitted chain letter . . . Until, once or twice a year, from the white belly there bursts forth a flower. This sheet of rose-pink laid paper, for example, perfumed with violets, which starts without preamble: "O Angel, my Archangel!"

Archangel, do you realize! With a capital letter! One of the Thrones, the Dominations! One of Those who Soar among the Clouds! There was no doubt at all that it meant me, for my name was there on the envelope, all in feminine flourishes but none the less as firm as the tread of the Theban Legion!

It must be a joke, I thought, nothing but a joke, but first let's read what it says . . . And my eyes flew at once to the signature, only to find, alas, a sort of Gordian knot, a deliberate scribble; the signature, in short, to an anonymous letter.

When the girls had their heads bent over their essays and I had a chance to read it, the letter ran as follows.

O Angel, my Archangel! Tell you I must: I love you! And do not think me brazen, for you will never know my name. Although, even shielded by anonymity, I tremble. Ten times have I picked up my pen before taking the plunge. In the end I had to do it: this secret weighed too heavily upon me. And besides, the school year is ending, it is time to say goodbye, it is time to purge one's heart. O Angel, my Archangel! Before I knew you I was afraid of happiness. You have changed my being, you have lifted the mourning from my soul. This you must know, O best beloved. And you must know that in my diary, between the pages for the 21st and 22nd of June, between St Paolino of Nola and St Aloysius Gonzaga (may they both watch over you), I keep your photograph, the group photograph taken in the gym, with you standing there, the headmaster at your side. I can't be seen in the photograph, because I hid behind you to gaze upon the nape of your neck, the little brown mole that bides there. My handsome, handsome husband, I know you write poetry. Then write a poem for me, for the unknown beauty (for such I am!) who loves you! I kiss you on both eyes.

A joke of course. Iaccarino's work. Only he could have thought up a cock-and-bull story of that sort. Probably to take my mind off Maria Venera. Even so, granted the unlikelihood of those lines being genuine, I felt strangely touched by them; I was grateful to whoever had written them for having written them. I will go further: they arrived at the right moment, while I was preparing to humiliate myself as Maria Venera's accomplice, with no hope of more than a nod of thanks. If it was indeed a game, I hoped that it wouldn't end, that the correspondence would continue; so acutely, at that time, did I feel the need for some amorous illusion. Let Venera, Venera the idol, strew her incense on others from a bounteous censer, for now it mattered little. If not hers, another womanly aroma, true or false as it might be, had come to titillate my nostrils.

I therefore stepped down and walked to and fro between the

desks, glancing to right and to left, for you never know. Every so often I nodded in answer to an imaginary question, cheered by the good omens and gladsome smiles of fortune which were bringing such unexpected and agreeable turmoil into my life.

For you must know that, years before, I had travelled much amid blood and tears, and my legs still ached from it. I had missed my youth as one misses a train, and in its place there remained in my mind a deep, dark gulf, that I camouflaged to no avail with brushwood and disguised with flowers. I knew it was still there, scar of the unhappened, gash of the unlived. I felt it every evening on my cheek, smarting more than a slash from Zorro. Well now, it seemed the wheel was moving the other way. Now, turning thirty, I surprised myself, a boy among boys, encountering the unplayed games of love and chance in a light of wonder.

There was more to come. When I left the classroom with my briefcase full of homework, and an expression, no doubt, somewhere between the dazed and the debonair, a sullen Galfo was waiting for me in the corridor. It was I who had summoned him, on the telephone during break. I was to tell him, from Venera, to give up on the whole business, but he forestalled me. He had heard I was teaching the girl and, he said, playing the lover-boy, and he told me to lay off.

"Lay off yourself," I retorted. "Venera doesn't want either of us. As for the baby, that'll be managed somehow."

He turned white, then red, and came at me with his fists. My laugh made no impression on him. He meant to challenge me, he hissed. This evening, with bare fists, up at the Belvedere, unless I dared to accept other weapons against him; he, who was an infallible butcher of ringdoves and woodcock. I watched him talk, and my heart bled for him. He was so incensed, but also sad, muddled, in need of help. In the end, not knowing what to answer, I said I wanted neither fists nor firearms, they were all Greek to me, and at most I could accept a game of draughts, the loser to pay for the coffee. He lost control, but the hand he suddenly raised in an attempt to slap my face luckily got wedged between my briefcase and the class register, which I had raised as a shield. Nor did Ermenegilda, hurrying to the scene, have any trouble in separating us, taking his arm and bearing him off to her sanctum. Whither I myself followed at once, to console him and to mop with my handkerchief at the huge and prodigal tears of his desolation.

I was late for lunch, but Iaccarino and Licausi had waited on for me in the restaurant. I saw them scanning me as I entered, their eyes aglow with wine and faces flushed with digestive effort. They were in the grip of palpable excitement; even the fish seemed to share it, redoubling its buttings and lashings against the panes of its prison. It was clear they expected me to furnish the most detailed reports, both on yesterday's meeting with Venera and on today's clash with Galfo, the rumour of which had already spread, and beaten me to it. I kept them in suspense, wanting a quiet bite first; and making a point of choosing, as a private allusion, that ultra-fine spaghetti which goes by the name of "Angel's Hair". Then, having summoned Mariccia to join the consultation, now that the last customer had left, I recounted everything from A to Y, stopping short only of the Z of the incipient motherhood.

As was to be expected, the sufferings of the dancing-man aroused no one's sympathy, and concerning the affair of honour the audience was pitilessly ribald. The suggestions were many: that I should meet him up on the Belvedere with Mambrino's basin on my head and a wooden Durendal, crying "Have at thee now!" from afar; that the pair of them should follow me swathed in white sheets, and suddenly jump out wailing "Ooooh, hoooh!"; that we should have invitations to the duel printed at Matteo Baglieri's, as for a wedding, and publicly distributed to all the Squires and Dames . . .

Frivolities, these, that somewhat damped my ardour. I had been the first to laugh at Galfo's challenge, but all the same, in my heart of hearts, I would have liked my friends to take it seriously. I wanted to wallow in pulsing rhythms and a fanfare or two. A life with a lilt to it, more *opera buffa* than Grand, but at least with me in the tenor lead. But instead all I got was this comic interlude, with the added irritation, as regards my love for Venera, that my friends did not display due solidarity and consideration. They had no doubt about it: I would merely be her plaything; worse still, her amatorial postman. They maintained that she was an out-and-out slyboots, mixed up and mad about men, but scatterbrained. So they said, and for a moment or two I agreed with them. Then Venera once again became, in my eyes, on a par with the Madonna of Gulfi, she who came from over the sea, and not even three yoke of oxen could budge her from the site where she had resolved to stop and have an altar set up. A site, without the shadow of a doubt, that in Venera's case would be my heart.

I was even more stung by the fact that none of them thought me capable of exciting love. The letter to Angel Archangel, if it was a hoax (and it could be nothing else), was in itself the proof of this. People don't play pranks like that on Don Giovanni, only on Leporello . . .

To stoke up my own convictions I drew out the page perfumed with violets and read it aloud, twice, first making each of them sniff at it, much as they rub the muzzles of police dogs with the knickers of the vanished damsel. The comment when I finished was an exclamation halfway between amazement and raillery. I ignored it and started to work on Iaccarino, determined to lure him into the open.

"Did *you* write it?"

I was not expecting a direct answer. Iaccarino was incapable of engaging in colloquy without its turning on his tongue into magniloquence. Especially at table, when he had dipped too often into the pitcher of Cerasuolo, the custom was that once he had been presented with an argument he would pull the cook onto his knee, ruffle her towy old mop of hair, and go off on a jaunt of words. So it was now, and the prating twaddle he concocted ran more or less like this.

"There are many ways, both oral and manual, of transmitting thought, but the most ancient and estimable is the unsigned letter. Immune from all belletristic ambition, a veridical voice from out the abyss, it is of all existing things the most propinquant to the word of God."

"You're forgetting thunder," I objected. "*Coelo tonantem* . . .", while Licausi, who in our concert-parties had elected to sing a humble ground-bass, and whom Iaccarino therefore dubbed "my Sancho", simply mouthed a "Bang!"

Quite out of her depth, Mariccia giggled, so that Iaccarino lost patience and pushed her off him. Then, in pedagogical tones, he continued: "I'm not forgetting it. It is an accepted fact that creation is nothing but a Bang, an awe-inspiring rumble in the belly of Who-Knows-Who. A rumble, but to my nose a surreptitious fart, a catafart, an anonymous codex, an unsigned crime, like the ones your Sherlocks clumsily toil to decipher. In a word, no less than anonymous paintings, and foundlings on the convent doorstep, the fatherless letter is a relatively sublime form of bastardy, of which it is worth our while to classify the species."

He made a complacent pause, in case we tried to contradict him. Instead, I buttered him up with "You talk like a dream," and poured him out another glass of wine.

"In anonymous writings," he went on, "you will distinguish three distinct genres, though they are sister genres. The first of these aims at intimidation, at incrimination, and proceeds from downright bile. Assertive and forceful, it is frugal with words: MENE TEKEL UPHARSIN, or YOU ARE A FOOL. The second feeds on doubts and fears, divulges hopes and secrets, exudes languishing and long-winded humours. An example of this, violet scented, you have in your hand. But the third, the most meritorious, broadcasts bitter, salutiferous truths, opens the eyes of the judges, and above all of husbands . . ."

Pandering to his mania for quotations and whims of speech, well knowing what acrimony and heartache they concealed, "Othello," I apostrophized, "Othello,

Know'st thou what Desdemona was about
Whilst thou in the Arsenal did'st black thyself
With sticky pitch?"

I was giving him rope to hang himself, but never letting him pause without pouncing: "*Did* you write it?"

He took no notice; he was in full spate.

"O dispatch arriving at dawn with the soft pace of the postman, scented with precious essences, umbrageously do you conceal yourself; you do not caw but coo, and rather than proclaiming you insinuate . . . Exemplary flea in the ear, miner's lanthorn, blind man's pathfinding staff! You it is who raise the unsullied stone to reveal beneath it the swarms of pallid millipedes; you who, unheeded, premonish Caesar of the Ides of March; you who . . . Indeed, no wonder your worshipful parent is said to be Master Crow, the wisest of all animals!"

"Objection, Your Honour, " I interrupted. "Call to mind the lines we learnt at school, '*Maître Corbeau sur un arbre perché* . . .'

"Objection overruled," replied he. "For every doltish crow that sits in a tree and eats with its beak open, a thousand far wiser ravens fast atop the busts of goddesses and croak 'Nevermore'."

Mariccia, who in such straits as these lost patience after three minutes (exactly three minutes after me), attempted to stem the tide.

"Crows or no crows, let me tell you I think this letter stinks. Could any woman, however brainless, take *him* for an archangel?" And she jerked a thumb at me in cheerful disdain. "But if she's on the level – and mind you I don't believe it – I bet she's ashamed to own up to such silliness and put her name to it."

"When women go buying onions at the market," sneered Licausi, "they wear veils."

I had them all against me now, so I gave a nudge of encouragement to the blind man who had just that moment arrived; he came in every day with his accordion to assist the peristalsis of us messmates. But Iaccarino had not yet finished blazing away. His yell, as he commanded silence, struck terror into the poor bastard, who had already embarked on *Sciuri sciuriddu*.

"If I were marooned on a desert island," he pontificated, "I should wish for no book other than a dictionary. Such are the outcries and oratorios to be heard in its dizzying entrails. In the same way it is likely that all the anonymous letters scattered throughout the world are the fragmented words of a single Leviathan letter written by a single hand, a single hidden Crow, in order to enshrine therein an Absolute Meaning. On its own, this little note of yours counts for no more than one of the thousands of potsherds into which Phidias' Zeus was smashed, but if you piece it together with the others, with all the sundered members, you will see that it will answer. For the answer exists, a shadow of the Word surviving among the syllables of Babel. Or possibly only a momentary incarnation of Proteus . . . Do you know how many are the faces of Proteus? Incalculable numbers, and each disavows the next, and both is and is not Proteus. Therefore I ask myself, I ask you: the true, unsundered Proteus, where is he?"

In spite of the zest he seemed to be putting into it, it was plain at this point that he was talking through his hat, out of maudlin drunkenness. So I made a dash for the door; I was expected by Venera and her pregnancy troubles. But first, to get it off my chest, "I know perfectly well you wrote it!" I bluffed from the doorway. As a result of which he finally made up his mind, pulled a face and drawled, "Of course, of course. Copyright by Iaccarino." Which was maybe an admission, maybe just the last word in leg-pulls.

SECOND ASIDE

Portrait of the artist as a young pennywhistle.

Another pause, if you please. At this point I would like to present myself as I was then; I may not yet have done so sufficiently well. I was at that time a pennywhistle capable of only two notes. Easy enough to play, but I had to be learnt. The notes were two, one of woe, *yelp yelp*, like a dog taking a beating; the other of bliss, *tralala tralalera*, brought on by my gusto for every piping-hot, red, meaty ragù of life – a gusto which not even thirty years of pincers and torn-out toenails have been able to impair. Two notes. Two alternating notes I heard my lips pipe according to the seasons. In the equinoctial months my thoughts ran on dying, I nicknamed myself Gingolph the Forsaken, title of an old pulp novelette by heaven knows whom, and each morning on waking I asked myself whether I was aught but a loathly worm, a spent cartridge, flotsam on the profluvium of the millennia. What little good or ill I did, thought, or suffered, the infinitesimal stirring of vice or of virtue which made my nerves vibrate for an instant . . . what could these matter, and to whom? For, were it possible, and with an immense margin of error I thought that it was possible, to calculate how many thousands of millions of men had so far inhabited the earth, and the innumerable ways they had died: phthisis, epilepsy, syphilis and leprosy, meningitis, carcinosis, ague and the plague; rat-bite, buzzard-bite, jackal-bite, dragon-bite; sword-cut, spear-thrust, bullet-hole, bomb; salt-water nightcap, combustion of bonfires, tumbles from clifftops, trapezes in circuses, windows in Prague; cachexy, apoplexy, malady, infirmity . . . or the unexpected shattering of the heart . . . if one could reckon the number, greater still by far, of the stirrings and throbbings of feeling in each of the lives ever lived: the yearnings, the jealousies, the torments, the terrors, the passions, the compassions . . . if there were a record of all the couplings of humans and amorous whisperings in grottoes and graveyards, bowers and bedrooms, booths in bars and the backseats of cars . . . summing up with the fact that time has turned all this to nothing and the least part of nothing, while once more, to no purpose, a flash of quick light is repeated in me . . .

And dwelling on this last, behold to my aid springs all the vigour and benevolence of the solstice, the glory of it, the tart savour of its sea-breezes. This was my time to go chanting *tralala tralalera*, feeling the nip of it in my veins and nostrils. Where were the shrinkings and the glooms of yesterday? From one day to the next I was a different man; no walls could hold me still. An exorcism had sufficed to heal me, a small word whispered in my ear by the sun. Like a snake reviving in the quarantine of its winter quarters, I found every funnel of a den too cramped for the abundance of my coils.

If I look at myself in the snapshots of that time (6 × 9 prints from a Kodak Brownie), my expression is one of jovial alarm, in which the two natures, the two notes, pipe together: the finicky and the easy-going, the whimper and the warble. I remember Iaccarino saying once, "The day will come when one of us will learn of the other's death. And then this moment we are living through together, and together we will both remember as long as we live, will be cut by half, pilfered of fifty per cent. At last the black tide will cover the survivor, and there will be no one left to know that at half past one in the afternoon, on July the 13th 1951, in front of the Turco-Colosi news-stand, we lit two Serraglios with the same match . . ."

A long way round indeed, just to cadge a cigarette, but I was moved all the same. I learnt for the first time to distinguish plural memories from solo ones, and of how we die every day with the deaths of those who remember us, and how every day we kill others by forgetting them.

A long, long time has passed. Today, if I try to whistle, the hiss that escapes through this gap in my teeth, here where two incisors are missing, doesn't mean a thing. I have no longer friends nor fairy-tales; all I do is compose cabals and cabalettas of words, diddles and brabbles of words to hoodwink death. I write to you, *desocupado lector*, blind, voiceless face, white mist between me and my portable, but verily I do not love you, and would prefer no one to watch as I kick my legs about ever more dog-weary in my *Ballo di Sfessania*. Fricasso, Scaramucia, Frittellino, brothers in Christ . . . I am the clown on stilts in the background, who looks like falling, who must fall from one moment to the next.

Let's try it once again: *yelp yelp, tralala* . . . Once again it all ends in a fit of coughing, and the Papageno I used to be puerilely puffs out his cheeks in vain. Write? Of course. Live? No. I write the beginnings of books that will never get written. I ponder openings in the style of *Hellzapoppin'*, the vagaries of desperation: "Ignazio Sanchez left home at five o'clock to take tea"; "The marquesa left home at five to go to the bullfight"; "At five in the afternoon the marquesa went out with Ignazio" . . . I write apathetic eulogies of the inkstain on my right thumb; I write to God, though discretion enjoins me to secrecy; I write to Caesar: "Divine Caesar, your *retiarius* writes to you. *Ave, Caesar, scripturus te salutat* . . ." I write to the clouds over Ammazzanuvole, to the winds that carried them off . . .

If only I *enjoyed* writing! Instead I drag my pen like a gammy leg, I plough the paper as a bitter purgative and penitence. This miracle of producing with a few sounds and signs a bubble of garrulous humbug, how often, how endlessly it seems underhand and contemptible. Although I try to make a joke of it, a pastime, to hasten along what minutes of future have been imposed on me; although instead of memories I find myself recounting a dream, or spinning a yarn, the taste it leaves is always toxic. It's like Grock's dialogue with the doctor: "Cure me, doctor, I'm unhappy." "Go to the circus and see Grock." "I can't. I *am* Grock."

Alas, poor Grock! Alas, poor Gesualdo! Perhaps I should give only my name and number, refuse to open my mouth, invoke the Geneva Convention on prisoners-of-war . . .

Then again, no. In the country a big walnut tree is growing despite me, its roots threatening the walls of my neighbour's house. Some time ago I embedded it in cement both wide and deep, I thrust it into a strait-jacket, I clamped down on the old trunk to teach it to be good. This morning a bump in the cement, a suspect crack, tell me that the root has not surrendered, that it journeys on . . .

So *tralala tralalera*, pipe up Papageno!

SEVEN

The Clubs of the Far South. Afternoon and evening with Sasà Trubia.

We had fixed the day, Venera and I, but the expedition to Catania proved unnecessary. An hour before leaving, in the process (*horribile dictu!*) of sweeping the landing in place of Anita, Maria Venera took a tumble, more or less on purpose, down all twenty-seven steps to street level, and found herself, with no need for forceps, miscarried and glad of it. She shared the news with me from the ottoman where she lay, recovering from her bruises and everything else. A heaven-sent tumble, she confided, for although it would keep her out of action for two weeks, it had come at just the right moment to provide a natural substitute for a dangerous business. I was equally glad, if only for the money I'd save, since I'd made up my mind to pay the *faiseurs d'anges* out of my own slim pocket. I was much less glad about the sudden coldness of the girl, now that she had no further use for me. She declared herself reluctant to go on with her studies, thus jeopardizing my legitimate chance of seeing her daily. Moreover, whether from carelessness or malice I know not, amongst so many familiar *tu*'s, long sanctioned by usage, she dropped a cold-shouldering *lei* and failed to correct it. I admit she continued to call me by my first name; as if, however, to utter its three syllables turned her stomach. And must I tell all? She allowed me to find her one afternoon in her dressing-gown, with her hair in curlers.

Apart from that, her whole attitude seemed to have changed, and with such off-hand breeziness, that is, without any preliminaries to this volte-face, that I came to agree with Iaccarino that she was a common or garden slyboots with a woolly head, unable to see beyond the end of her nose and not clever enough to be an egoist of real class.

What was I to do? I gave back chill for chill, telling her I had posted the package, but that another time she could make other arrangements. As for the lessons, very well, that was her business: all the more free time for me. Finally, while fishing cigarettes out of my pocket, I nonchalantly let drop the letter to Angel Archangel; and I took my leave at once.

Schoolboy tricks, of course. As if a girl like Venera could get jealous over someone she didn't love. All the same, the thought that she would read all those burning words addressed to me tickled my downcast vanity. Not to mention that the mislaid letter would be a good excuse to return . . .

Back in Lower Módica, boredom led my steps to the Conservative Club. A club for the bigwigs, this, where we teachers gained access only by virtue of the franchise customarily extended by such places to guests from out of town. The three of us, and myself in particular, were glad to go there, for reasons which I will shortly explain.

The Clubs of the Far South have a bad reputation. Haunts of sloth and idleness, it is said, where amidst the click of cannoning billiard-balls, the rustle of newspapers clipped in wooden holders, and the moans of landowning weather-prophets, the years, and the seats of trousers, are consumed away, and lives moulder in interminable repeat performances.

This is a half-truth only. Just as much they provide a stage for pantomime and creative tittle-tattle. Something akin to church-steps in the days of the Medici, swarming with raconteurs; or to those Georgic nights on the banks of the Po, when until a few years ago they would weave many a ring o' ring of roses of verbal drollery. Not otherwise had the Conservative Club in Módica set up as a non-stop city music-hall, lacking only a box-office at the entrance and an attendant to take the money, so rife were the quips and cracks extemporized now by one now by another of the members, egged on by an invisible call-boy from three in the afternoon until nine in the evening. Ear-splitting at times, as they sat in the baccarat room where age-old fortunes fell headlong in the course of a single hand; under the breath at others, as they stood unseen at the shutters, observing the evening promenade up and down the Corso and harkening to the indefatigable heartbeat of existence.

That moment was the fountain-head of some truly grandiose rumours and slanders, the underpinning of the fantasy framework on which the comedy of the town flourished day by day, a performance in perpetual motion in which everyone was simultaneously spectator, actor, author and impresario . . .

If anything leapt to the eye of an outsider, in fact, it was the ease with which, within those walls, every respectable Tom, Dick, or Harry, however firmly encased in the shell of his municipal or social identity, was made to drop all that, and play the puppet of himself, a string-dancing Punchinello or chattering Pinocchio. It took but a barely perceptible oddity of speech or gesture, the most trifling quirk of character, of conduct, of dress, and that habit, enhanced by the loquacious clairvoyance of the others, would at once become a hallmark, the lethal thumbsketch of some mania or other. What is more, it seemed that by dint of seeing themselves mirrored in the opinions of their neighbours, people felt obliged to match up to the mask imposed on them, be it jocund or funereal, and to sew it to their skin like a second, more authentic identity. With effects of comical distress that can readily be imagined.

The first time I entered that hall of masks they rather clipped my wings, marking me down as a studious little schoolteacher, accustomed to ambling about on foot with armfuls of tattered books – a Socialist, maybe, or even an Anarchist . . . but, in the last analysis, a pusillanimous scarecrow.

I can't say they were wrong to have rated me thus. Those were days when I used to blush easily, and hot flushes would rush abruptly from one ear to the other, curse them! Much as I had felt at the army medical, naked against a whitewashed wall. A feather in my cap, therefore, was my recent exploit in pursuit of Maria Venera, which seemed to have changed my status, and turned on all the searchlights in town to probe beneath my greasepaint poultice for the features of a *miles gloriosus*. Yes, it was a feather in my cap, and stirred in me a modest pride, and in my heart some hopes. Maybe – I don't say Venera, on whom by now I counted very little, but maybe those other thousand girls, nameless in the shadows, whom I might love at any moment, were waiting only for their ears to ring with my lusty cock-a-doodle-doo. Or maybe not, maybe they didn't give it a thought. For me, however, some such make-believe could serve all summer. For life is not only fun to live; it is almost as much fun to fake it and fib it.

Anyway, what I needed was some kind of *laisser-passer* for the imminent festivities. In the drawing-rooms of the smart set grand manoeuvres were in preparation for July and August. The calendar was stuffed with them. Rumour told of dressmakers plagued by the most marriageable of the marriageable, of spindrift confections bespoke from Paris, of antique pendants exhumed from the family coffers. There would be much dancing on the terraces of the big mansions up at La Sorda, in the chalets of Sampieri, in the great garden at Chiaramonte, which a committee of gentlewomen had commandeered for the Gala Ball (by special invitation only). To which I, who had only attended a handful of Christmas parties in middle-class and well-to-do families, was doubtful of being invited unless someone gave me a hand. I feared, I very much feared, that the music and the lanterns, the alabaster of moons and of bosoms, the black feather boas round necks priceless with gems, the whispers and tremulous raptures of love, would languish upon the silver salver untouched by the lips of this thirsting lackpurse.

I know now, and I knew then, that I was paying court to a fantasy. The local aristocracy was a mere daub in comparison with the glamour that enchanted me in books. All the same, as in a pavement-artist's copy some glimmer of Raphael survives, or some shadow of Mozart even in the worst performance, so, when I witnessed Giuliana di Giardinello descending from her father's Fiat Balilla, which she drove with kid-gloved hands, or saw Donna Malide Tuscano turn in the stage-box to survey the stalls through her lorgnette, I will not say that my heart missed a beat, but a perturbation seized me, as if in the Champs Elysées or at the Opéra I had seen approaching the plumed headgear of the Baronesse Nucingen or the Duchesse de Guermantes.

What is more, now that I was in the doldrums with Venera, and my love for her was like a fire havering between becoming a blaze or dying down, my relations with society took on a more urgent belligerency. These were the lists where I was destined to win or to lose, not only my assay with women and love, but also, and more basic, my battles with myself and the world.

And so: "Módica, my gauntlet!" said I, only half in jest and stamping my foot. And, having left a message for Madama that I would be home late or nevermore, I set off with martial step to cross the threshold of the Conservative Club.

My intention was, for the moment, to practise some gentle diplomacy. Not all military triumphs start with an invasion, and my first need was to achieve some alliance and advocacy in social circles. I knew that the master of ceremonies for the forthcoming attractions, the Doge of the licit and illicit pleasures of Módica, the man, in a word, who arranged the invitations as he saw fit, was Don Nitto Barreca, a notorious party-organizer and gamester, always ready to sit up half the night, despite the fact that he did the rounds with his scoliotic neck supported by a plaster gorget. He fancied himself as an authority on antiques, and was suspected of illegal excavating, and worse; but I had once told him the difference between black-figure pottery and red-figure pottery, and he had been grateful. I therefore had hopes of his patronage, but sought him in vain in the inner room, because the baccarat session had been put off until the following day. Instead I was greeted with a curious smile by Trubia, as he raised his head from the billiard table and his game against a young man with foreign clothes and accent. A

Frenchman by the name of Michel, in our midst on behalf of Jean Renoir, no less, and on the lookout for locations for a film based on a story by Mérimée. Imagine! I was wild with excitement. Was Renoir coming? Anna Magnani? The Frenchman let us have it from a height, squashingly: "*Ça dépend, ça dépend.*" And down went the head for the next cannon. Until Trubia raised his hands in token of defeat and asked us up to his place, just around the corner, to have a drink and hear his new jazz records.

It was a beautiful evening. Through the open window came the sounds of the "Salon" like a background murmur of applause for the concert we were listening to. *Too-too-tootle-ooo* riffed the trumpet of Cootie Williams, and brought a lump to my throat that would go neither up nor down.

The Frenchman, from sheer patriotism, liked Bechet's *Careless Love*, because Claude Luther was in it (he said he knew him, they'd had a girl together), but I wanted to listen three times over to Charlie Parker, *Relaxin' at Camarillo*, which Sasà told me had been composed in a home for nervous diseases. Next on the list, *Saint James' Infirmary*, a lament over more humble calamities, gave me a chance to make a comparison between public hospitals and private clinics, the miseries of the flesh and the misfortunes of the mind, which would have been just up Iaccarino's street.

Trubia, seated beside the gramophone, busied himself changing records and needles, the perfect host. Between numbers I got up to make a closer inspection of the antique furniture, the pretty knick-knacks on the cabinet, the porcelain statuettes, the incongruous spinet in one corner. It was not design but accident that led me to spot Venera's envelope, empty, with the seals broken, among the other rubbish in the wastepaper basket; but it was no accident if, standing by the desk while Sasà and Michel, eyes closed, were savouring a joky trombone solo, I reached out to rummage through his recent mail and there, not without a pizzicato of secret laughter, came across a photograph of Sasà, bearded and curly-haired, to whose forehead a familiar green ink had added a pair of horns. A retrospective insult? A menacing promise? *Too-too-tootle-ooo*, I laughed up my sleeve, tore my eyes away and returned to the others, ready to give my heart once more to the music. That's the young all over: they can switch feelings in a flash.

Michel had a fancy to dip into the local lore concerning spells and superstitions, and it fell to me to act as guide to the cave-like dwelling of Donna Tònchila the sorceress. She was a spirited, jolly old hag, who'd taken a liking to me ever since I started visiting her to learn about life and miracles. She had frequently offered to make me a love potion to win round whomever I pleased, withdrawing the offer only when I told her teasingly that I wanted the love of no creature of flesh and blood, but one of her own sprites, some daughter of Beelzebub squatting on the skylight of her hovel.

"I have no dealings with the *masters of the place*," said Tònchila with perfect seriousness, crossing herself. But Michel, who, in earnest or in jest, had asked for something to soften an over-coy photographer-girl in his troupe, was made to pay through the nose for the powder and mumbo-jumbo designed to bring the shrew to heel.

Time had flown meanwhile, and the Frenchman had to leave us. Trubia invited me to dinner at a gourmet restaurant in Upper Módica. "I'll tell him, I'll tell him not," I said over and over to myself. Exactly what, I didn't know. I only knew I had a vague urge to bring the conversation round to Venera, watch his reactions, and thereby interpret the girl's true feelings and (why not?) my own as well. As things went, I didn't open my mouth all through the meal, and he showed no inclination to talk about anything except his latest run of bad luck at the tables and the revenge he would indubitably take tomorrow.

"I'll come along too," I promised, confident that I'd see Don Nitto there. And we sauntered off together to the cinema to see a digestive Napoleonic movie.

The lovely Adalgisa smiled on him alone as she tore off the tickets. I went ahead and stood behind the back row, lurking by the ruby-red curtain until my eyes had grown accustomed to the darkness. When I was able to bag the first free seat, and yield my willing neck to the plush of the seat-back, lo and behold on the screen was the Old Guard drawn up in a square, and the crackle of gunfire and an aura of dust and glory . . . At which point my eyelids could hold up no longer; they closed, leaving me to mull over for the umpteenth time the many setbacks of my life. How many things gone haywire, Lord knows! How many rebuffs, daily and yearly. That Me I dreamt of – telescope slung round the neck, right hand in feigned repose between third and fourth buttonhole of turquoise *redingote*, watching the sun rise between two steeples at Austerlitz – how come I find him here with a full belly, intent only on the internal coitus between enzymes, juices and papillae after a copious meal; a gormless orchestral finale, in which the basso continuo is the dried-dung cigar offered me by Sasà, my insipid Seraglios left neglected . . . There! All it took was a plutocratic forty winks and I think no more of my battles; even of ungrateful Venera I think no more!

The lights came on, my eyes came open; the first reel was home and dry. In one of the front rows, beside the black curls of a girl-friend, I caught a glimpse of the tresses of Isolina, blacker yet; and behind her, Licausi smoking like a chimney, pretending to observe the antics of flies in the air.

EIGHT

A word on happiness.
Presenting Don Nitto.
Cards at the Conservative Club.

"Licausi has a heart *à la coque*, incapable of extreme emotion." Thus Iaccarino, when I told him the latest.

Yet signs to the contrary were multiplying. Already Licausi only showed up at mealtimes, alternately taciturn and talkative but always inopportunely so. Assuming his heart to be an egg, it was plainly not just coddled but overcooked; I was up in these things. Mariccia agreed with me, at the same time handing me a note that Puck had brought. It was from Venera.

The crazy girl had changed her mind and wanted to go back to her studies. I ranted, I relented, I returned. She settled down to it seriously this time, avidly drinking in my elucidations; though at the same time her pen meandered over the paper, less for note-taking than for green-ink doodles complete with tails and horns and labelled SASÀ. In the end we laughed over them together, for by this time she was perfectly open about it.

"Commit murder? Commit suicide? What do you advise?"

"Why not both, first one and then the other?" I replied flippantly, but not without a pang in the solar plexus, of solicitude for her, mortification for myself, envy for Trubia. At moments such as these I began to think about the jumbled paste-up of my future. "I want happiness," I had decided on the previous New Year's Day. "For a month or for an hour, I want it!" But, after all, what on earth *was* happiness? At one time I had thought it was born of loving. Then, of being loved. I now persuaded myself that the flower was nigh to blooming, ready for my fingertips to pluck, like the first almond for Licausi's hand that morning of the bet. Or wasn't happiness a feeling, maybe, of suspended time, of time immobile and golden? The illusion, that is, that the sun is stone-struck where it stands, and the moon likewise; that not a cell in our blood grows older by an instant, at this very instant that seems to pass but passes not, that seems never to pass but is past already. Oh to halt time, to suspend it, so that all things whatsoever, stone, fish, bird, leaf, fruit, and me and you Maria Venera, are all smitten by the light of a radiant, incorruptible Now; static, free of the undertow of our yesterdays dragging us down, foaming up over our lips; free of the reef of tomorrows bristling with spikes and knives, foreboding disaster and death; no past, no future, but the present only, and all of us blissful and beautiful, asleep in the wood, king, queen, and courtiers; and the princess, and even the prince himself, in an unalterable present, the selfsame golden revel of this June of 'Fifty-One.

Happiness, in short. What matter if it's paid me not in Spanish doubloons but in Weimar Deutschmarks? I have read in some book that the Rhine peters out in the sand before it reaches the sea. But first it runs, ah how it runs, blithesome and vagabond, through field and through forest, among rocks and trees, mirroring clouds and stars and the tresses of Undines ice-cold and laughing!

To flow in motionless time, though – is that ever possible? And vice versa, if all our wealth is words, and all our weaponry, how to bring time to a stand? By writing it down perhaps? I therefore needed words, and maybe more adjectives than nouns. To war against the ossification of the world, and objects without excellence, acts without passion. Even as, when a child, I scoured the dictionary for them, and each as it emerged was a goddess rising from the sea. Invented words, suspended time: this is my recipe for happiness.

In fact, from early days on, my first years at school, I found it every Monday at a news-stand opposite the school gates, in the pages of a children's comic. Here I lost myself in the green fields behind Felix the Cat, the blue skies, the red roofs, an angel town where time was dead but dying was impossible. Since then every syllable of mine has sought for painted Arcadies, no grume of human presence, but a waterfall poised in air, a windmill with still sails, a sun-tamed lizard between two stones, a peace; a morning that will never turn to noon. With rolling hills down yonder, where the horizon timidly yields to the light, and a church-spire raises a finger to the sky, and a flock nibbles in silence by the wayside, and the sun floods through chinks in the foliage in slender, slanting columns, awakens pure colours, icy, dripping colours, Prussian blues, Vermeer yellows, shadows of sound, perfumes of enamoured grasses . . .

Very well, then: it was a similar feeling that I was yearning for, a month or a week of it, from a Venera, or a surrogate Venera, or a stranger met at a dancing-party . . .

What a curious thing it is: both are blind, happiness and love, but they don't get on together. Love is far from being a peace, and no good at all for stopping time: it only shortens or lengthens it. Besides, it clutters the mind with a gaggle of talkative phantoms, a movie-show of ads and fads, with one voice ceaselessly shouting *you, you, you*; another giving blow for blow with *me, me, me*! It has nothing in common, has love, with any notion of happiness. Except when it has not yet arrived, and we wait for it at the window, cultivating a weakness for it, and scenting its breath afar off like a herald of spring. Therefore, if I wanted to be happy, how could love help? Maybe not at all; but maybe I had a fancy to call upon both their blindnesses, to refuse to sever them, to lump them together under a single contraband name. Years later I was to learn from an eastern sage that happiness can be this: hearing a little girl singing on the road at night, after she has asked us the way. But at that time my young wolf's teeth could not let any little Red Riding Hood go away singing . . .

I add that it was summer, a June on the brink of July, Mediterranean. With a thunder of sun on one's head, blackened stubble beneath one's feet, like the stumps of gangrened limbs. An orchestra of such frenzied sensuality would be hard to conduct, with its 'cellos on heat, its lugubrious timpani longing for death. What a sorry, quicksilver destiny is ours in Sicily, to have so much blood to expend in veins so poor and sluggish, and the strength of dwarves to match the pride of gods . . . And you may say that all this is irrelevant, that I've strayed from the point, but it might perhaps explain why, as I left Maria Venera's that evening, I had set my heart on one thing and one thing only: to be elected to the privileged few, to be among the secret three hundred names of the guests on the hand-written list in Don Nitto Barreca's back trouser pocket.

Don Nitto Barreca, known as "Bezique", was the sole survivor of a wealthy family with property here in our county but resident in Palermo. Having in the course of a few years lost parents, uncles, and aunts, not always without bloodshed, he had come with the intention of staying a week to take stock of his abundant inheritance, but ended by pitching camp and putting down roots in the mansion at La Sorda. Here he would entertain now one female, now another, in rigid six-monthly shifts, by God! – mouth-watering tigresses imported from distant harems. He only came into town on the evenings when gambling was billed at the Club, he was so addicted to it. He would really have preferred games of skill, but after a few early attempts, he had one day dismissed his eager bridge-companions, declaring himself willing to make a fourth only to the Father, Son and Holy Ghost. After which he turned to baccarat, which is far more popular down here.

I was rather in awe of Don Nitto, but I also admired him in a muddle-headed way, though it irked me to see him always accompanied by a bodyguard from Palermo, a sort of enormous bull in corduroy. Nor was this the only thing which put him on another plane. At Christmas I had seen him holding a bank worth millions with positively insulting sang-froid, following each successful strike – and not because nature prompted it, but out of sheer brass – with a salvo of yawns which still further deformed a face outstanding for its bristly moles. His stocky figure, his receding chin, the loud striped suit which (sewn southern-style to the lapel) bore, withal, a tenacious mourning-button, the occasional stammer called upon to mask goodness knows what occult intentions, the unsightly armature that shored up his neck, all these conspired to give him a shady air drawn close about him, so that to acquire his confidence would need more nerve than to rob the Bank of England. Truth be told, rumour had it that his gambling was a front for nefarious goings-on, the smuggling of antiques, and more. But I couldn't believe it, couldn't believe anyone would commit crimes without being in need. Nor, one assumes, was it believed by any of the local "quality", since they kowtowed to him, and paid court to him, and invited him into their homes, having optimistically kidded themselves that his kept woman was merely a guest from the Continent. This, then, was the man with whom I had to ingratiate myself if I wished to enter the social whirl.

My first step was to take my stand in the outer room, where the players gathered to drink coffee until the whole company was assembled for the after-dinner session. This began at about nine, and lasted far into the night. It opened with an auction for the bank, which was a pure formality, since Don Nitto was always the highest bidder. The next move was to appoint a book-keeper willing to help the banker check the punts, to cash in and pay out. Now, it happened that Don Nitto's choice fell as a rule on a certain hunchbacked lawyer, a great one for inventing winning systems; one who, having tried them out in person at San Remo, no longer had a penny of his own to risk, and contented himself with taking a platonic share in the passions of others, happy just to handle chips and banknotes, and to enjoy the stench of deathly sweats transpiring, yea all but palpable, around the green-baize table beneath the great cut-glass chandelier.

It was my intention to get rid of this man and take his place; and this I achieved by accidentally jogging the arm which supported his cup, bespattering his jacket at point-blank range with a large black coffee. The scalded and infuriated jurist hurried off to his wife for a change of clothes, passing Don Nitto in the street outside. On his arrival the latter, in the absence of any other takers, was forced to enlist yours truly; and I had the infernal gall to feign reluctance, to accept only as a personal favour.

When the customary green-baize cloth had been spread over three tables arranged in a row, the game began, with Don Nitto holding the bank, myself as cashier, and Ciccio Calafiore and Sasà Trubia at the two *tableaux*. With a crowd of others, of course, punting against the bank in the wake of these. This Calafiore was a nasty little carrot-top, stingy and hypocritical, who drew his cards with maddening languor, then either went down or demanded a card with a brusque monosyllable. Capable, when he was ahead of the game, of lurking in the lavatory on a spurious pretext, then creeping surreptitiously away. But Sasà was a player of nobler stamp, glancing nonchalantly at his cards and smiling or laughing when he lost. Except tonight, and the fact gave me food for thought. With such sullen love of self-destruction did he insist on making wrong bets, doubling or trebling his stake when everything advised the opposite. Luck, also, was meticulously hostile to him, so that little by little the fellow-punters at his *tableau* left him in the lurch and transferred their chips to the other side of the table, where Calafiore was to some extent holding his own. After the umpteenth loss (a resounding zero, in our jargon *pupa su pupa*, or court-card on court-card), Sasà began to bet on credit.

"Chalking up a thousand, a thousand to lose."

Twice, three times, each time knitting his brows more fiercely. Until, "I can't see the colour of your money," said Don Nitto, and Sasà shot to his feet, wrote a cheque for his debt, handed it to me, gave goodnight to the crowd, and away. Leaving me with a pricking doubt in mind, as to whether his mood arose from the distressing mail he had received from Venera, or whether perhaps his bad luck itself didn't stem from it. It is no rare thing for a person to cast the evil eye upon himself.

With a glance at Sasà's departing back, "*Une chandelle est morte*," said Don Nitto. Not only did he know all the games but the verbal liturgies that went with them. The game dragged on for hours yet, in the same bewitched fashion. The bank won time after time, and I mechanically raked in the winnings, pensively – among so many brows aflame with furious ecstasy – wondering which of the queens on the cards looked most like Venera. I was not even aware that things were drawing to a close until Don Nitto, holding up a nine and a court-card between finger and thumb, exclaimed "*Zerilò*!" It was two in the morning, and I was faced with a mountain of cash and securities, beneath which I laboured to locate the ash-tray to stub out my fag.

The word *Zerilò*, an arcane injunction which Don Nitto was in the habit of pronouncing to prick fate to further efforts, as a jockey sets his spurs to his Barbary steed in the home straight, resounded in the smoke-laden silence with the tones of a *De Profundis*. His next words, "*Il y a une suite*," with which he signified that he was handing over the bank, seemed like an ironical signature to a death certificate. Any sequel was out of the question, since no one had two coins left to rub together. The game was over and the night began.

Outside the Club we stopped to sniff the night air. There was an acrid smell to it, pleasant enough, like burning brushwood. Almost as if, on disappearing, the sun's charred heart had left an enduring fumigation behind it. Or else someone in the fields still had a bonfire going. We inhaled it in great gulps. Then, while the rest of them went their ways hugging the walls and not looking back, Don Nitto thanked me briefly, raising his eyebrows when I humbly declined the two per cent commission which by ancient custom the winner offers to his non-playing assistant.

"Ah, I think I understand," he said, and added, "No offence meant." And taking me by the arm he led me as far as his car. Then he asked me how old I was.

"I thought of you as younger," he said. "I'm glad. I can't bear the under-thirties. I like people who've picked up a few calluses."

I nodded, but I thought to myself, romantic though I felt myself to be, that he didn't know a whore from a handsore . . .

And, waving a hand from the car window: "Get a new suit made," said he. "In a few days' time you'll be needing it."

THIRD ASIDE

Temporary well-being and variations on an old theme.

Reader, what can I say? A coincidence maybe, and I'm loath to admit it, but for the last few days I've been feeling better; my eyes, no sooner closed, no longer teem with that swarm of night-haunting locusts. I always sleep little, as you know, and that is not good; not in this moon-forsaken Rome.

My moon does not reach to me here, my Iblean, agrarian moon. Barefoot on parquet I seek it without hope, through the chinks of the roller-blind I seek it, while all the nettles of the vigil to come already sting at my eyelids. Oh, hypothalamus, incurable throb behind the eyeballs. With how many thousands of make-believe yesterdays do you besiege me! How I suffer the vast encumbrance of every yesterday, of my own and of others, of my own and of history, of all births and deaths and destinies . . .

I imagine a sentry of old, seated by the embers of his camp-fire, and with the eyes and ears of that man I await the Macedonian or Thracian fated to kill me. Then, in a trice, two thousand years later, I am drooping Austrian melancholies over a sill, I am Hans, or Klaus, I am sheltering from the sleet in a *Stube* on the embankment by the river, I am stirred when the brasses of the *Rosenkavalier* play a phrase I adore. These are my midnight carnivals, my movie-shows from Babel. But it would take but a few grammes of . . . let's see . . . dihydronitrophenilbenzodi-azepin – (syllables of prayer, secret name of God!) . . . It would take but a few globular capsules, crushed and carefully dissolved, not forgetting a note of apology to you, dear reader, who have been so kind . . .

And instead, wondrously, for several days I haven't thought

of it. Or just once in a while in passing, when darkness falls and I feel I must get out, but I can't decide where, whether to a cinema in Prati or to tour the city in the slowest Circle Line tram.

To sleep, barbiturically to sleep, to dream, perchance to die . . . But at one time they were sleepless nights that never ended. Terrible nights. Whereas now they do the world for me, so full of visitors and visages, my hand ever ready to snatch them and pin them to the pillow. I am forever switching the lights on and off, as if playing larks with darkness, playing hide-and-seek. Nor do I cease for an instant – passing off lies as memories, swopping memories for dreams, laying it on in colours thick and thin – to tell my story. My own amanuensis, what a stroke of luck . . . and I've got the job for life!

This morning, too, in the X-Ray unit waiting for a check-up, in this brief interim resting a sheet of paper on a fat copy of *Neuropathic News*, my nostrils seeking the once-familiar smell of emulsion and the crypt behind the dark curtains. I am a shade disappointed when, instead of the face of the Skinny Wizard, another, with different spectacles, comes peering out, and a different voice says "Strip off!"

I fall asleep and at last, and after so long and so long, I have a love-dream: she with faceless flesh, and I lie under, passive and possessed by her, swallowed up by a carnivorous plant, *Drosera rotundifolia*, the Sundew of my schoolbooks, consumed and imbibed by the valves of those innermost lips, a feverish corolla puckering and swelling unceasingly about me. Not so easy, after the pleasure of it, to grope with half-closed eyes and search out a change of underwear. But now it is done, and no more sleep for me. I shall wait upon the dawn, as ever, eavesdropping on the sonatas of darkness, the woodworm, the footsteps of shadows in the passage, the blather of wind in the funnel of the chimney . . . And the plaints of the scrumpled balls of newspaper I tossed onto the floor last night as I finished page by page before putting out the light. Prompted from within (I shall never know whether aiming at order or at chaos), at intervals throughout the night they crackle inexplicably.

I think back to Iacca's lectures: for he had made the choice, or so he thought, between design and disaster. But what about me? Some mornings, when I get up, a certain feeling of symmetry grabs hold of me; I surrender to it totally, as if I were the latest growth-ring in the trunk of a great tree; or, in a dutiful chain, a molecule. At such moments I have no doubt about it, that out of all the syllables in a dictionary, even jumbling them up and wedding them again at random, a child's hand could compose an Iliad, and the wind at least a Cumaean oracle. Why then, yesterday in the trolley-bus, that feeling of sinister delight when the twinge in my right hypochondrium told me that among my flock of fibres there was a rebel? Why that pique that borders on resentment every time any sort of gadget actually works for me? The loyalty of the nut to the bolt, the punctuality of the comets, the mathematical rule of three – nothing at such moments upsets me more. I think then of that point in the ocean where compasses are driven witless, and I wonder whether the enigma that concerns myself might not more easily be solved by blindness than clairvoyance.

But forgive me reader, I now return to you. I have to introduce you to Cecilia, sing her to you . . . Then we have the Ball Scene, then I make it rain, I make another season start, say farewell, go on my way.

NINE

Epiphany of Cecilia. Mariccia as barber. Divers counsels to a bachelor concerning marriage.

It was eight o'clock of an evening, an evening late in June, when the stupendous Cecilia made her début in the Corso. No one noticed. They were all gawking up at a trick-cyclist riding a high wire strung across from one palazzo to another. Even I, coming back from a lesson with Venera (Alvise, for some reason, keenly on the qui vive), was instantly enthralled by such an out-of-the-way attraction. Less scared of a fall, since in any case there was a net, than beguiled by the presentiment of an assumption, an ascent on high miraculous and absolute. So I was perfectly willing to lower my eyes, assured of seeing, when I raised them again, nothing but a tenantless wire a-tremble in the air, bereft of both cyclist and velocipede. Vanished, the pair of them! Swallowed up for ever by a sudden crack in the sky.

Thus, daring one of these truces of attention, engaged in staring prudently at my shoes, I was surprised to encounter, next to my shoddy leather ones, two others, feminine, fashioned in white shagreen, and for all the world like a pair of dainty, amorous doves. Next, travelling warily upwards with the eye, behold the slender ankles sheathed in ethereal silk, a skirt of blackest satin, a white organza blouse, one gloveless hand dangling at her side and, hey presto, in one fell swoop, the shapely bosom, the mellifluous throat, the stately profile set off and balanced by a coal-black chignon: Cecilia.

I was struck at once by her blend of pride and sweetness, and in such majesty of the flesh a touch of natural melancholy. The sort of melancholy, I mean, not born of ugly memories, or books, or jangled nerves, but of some innate cause, some dark, lethargic vein among the red circuits of the blood. Cecilia. And when she dropped her headscarf and we both bent down to retrieve it, and I oh-so-lightly brushed her fingers, I knew that my goose was cooked, and that I would love her all week long with eternal love, and adore her all my life for at least a fortnight.

I should add that almost at once I was calling her "Cecilia" in my thoughts, and not without reason. For some time it had been common knowledge in town that up at La Sorda, in the mastiff-guarded mansion, Don Nitto was entertaining his customary, six-monthly, Continental lady-friend. As scrumptious, said the postman, alone in having snatched a glimpse of her, as one of Valdemaro's Lovelies. In short, the tops. And since the postman could read, she had a name: Cecilia Marconi. And here she was, it could be none other, and when I raised to my nose the hand that had touched hers, I found it fragrant as the hand of a hairdresser . . . The crowd soon parted us, but now, what matter? In my copious heart she had entered and taken her place (there was room for her beside Maria Venera, there was room enough for a hundred). This white-shod queen off the last train in from Sheba, whose name was Cecilia Marconi.

Before lunch next day I confided in Mariccia, while she was giving me a shave in the store-room. Not the first time, this. Mariccia had a light hand and, behind her, a professional apprenticeship dating back to her colonial days, when her Wayfarer's Inn assured hairy sergeants on twenty-four hour passes from Fort Capuzzo of "complete service and a holiday to remember". By kind permission of Don Cesare, I gladly placed myself in her hands, partly for the pleasure of conversing with her, while she was lathering me, about her venerable sciatica and my own callow love-affairs. This time, however, I found her hostile, shocked by my emotional extravagances, as a miser is shocked by a needless expense even if someone else is paying. She didn't like my being hooked on someone new; she had grown attached to Maria Venera and my consequent laments as unrequited lover. I therefore seemed to her doubly forsworn; for on the one hand, with the girl, I was bent on action after so many months of stagnant belly-aching, and on the other was seriously contemplating supplanting her with a new flame. At this juncture, I appeared to Mariccia in such a bad light, as such an unexpectedly iniquitous libertine, that the razor quivered in her hand. Then, with a touch of contrition perhaps, or some quirk of her sensitive, down-to-earth nature, she couldn't resist giving me her own opinion of the fugitives, to get the weight off her chest. There are certain things, she whispered, to keep mum about even with one's nearest and dearest, but she'd have me know that the dancing-man was not so lacking as they said he was. "And what I know I know!" she declared slyly, hammering home the monosyllables. She went on, "Now, take that escapade of Venera's . . . Baffling! Mind-boggling! Believe me, there's more in that than meets the eye – a rebound, maybe, like at billiards . . . Or a second best . . . Just a kid's revenge. Unless . . ."

She stopped, her lips clamped tight, and I, my own mouth a bubble with lather, was unable to wrench from her the rest of the conjecture.

A little later, face dried, sticking-plastered, and stunningly scented with lavender water, at twelve-fifteen the sole and premature customer, I sat thoughtfully at the table in the restaurant while she plied to and fro laden with plates.

Broad bean soup, or vegetable purée? I ate up, and she bustled about with dishes, still chattering on, no longer about Venera but about me, how fickle I was, and why didn't I get married?

"*Mula tinta, muggheri tinta – tintu cu nun l'ha né bona né tinta.*" These sibylline words ("A mule may kick and a wife may shrill – But if you ain't got 'em you're worse off still", or words to that effect) did not remain mysterious for long. She went straight on to quote the backbiting at my expense that was starting to do the rounds of the town: that I thought too much about women, that I did my thinking out loud and made sure everybody heard me. Whereas, if I got fixed up once and for all . . .

And she started to sing the praises of Don Cesare's goods and chattels, houses in Íspica, fields teeming with water, and an only daughter, not pretty perhaps, but my! how clever she was. Hard-working too. Was she in my class at school? No?

"Too bad for both of you," she asserted roundly, hobbling away, halt with arthritis, towards the kitchen. I didn't hang around waiting for her to spout me more proverbs, mostly off the top of her head. Mariccia had a habit of concocting proverbs and making them mean two opposite things within twenty-four hours—I myself until a few days before had been putting up with the likes of "Single is Saintly", designed to inveigle me not into marriage but perpetual celibacy. Taking advantage, therefore, of her absence in the kitchen, and deftly avoiding getting tangled up in the chains of the fly-screen, I slipped away, leaving on its saucer the lone peach served me for dessert, uncut and in its dust-jacket.

My friends were no more sympathetic. Even Iaccarino, from whom I was expecting congratulations on my switch of direction, he who was dead-set against Maria Venera, was really peeved at this excess, this redoubling of my overflow of love, to the jeopardy of our communal larks and walks together. So much so that, feeling himself forsaken by both of us, both Licausi and me, he of all people started pleading the case for fidelity.

"I hate bigamy," he said. "Especially when it's platonic and all in the mind."

I didn't rise to the bait. Bigamist? Why not? Venera, after a day's eclipse, had reconquered my imagination and was there encamped, even though I now saw her every afternoon, no barrier between us but a grammar-book, prickly with aorists and duals, and I no longer needed to eavesdrop of an evening, beneath the balcony of her Bizet. She was always in my thoughts Maria Venera, nor did I cease to be initrigued by the sweet bedlam of her way of thinking, the everlasting mishmash of her hobgoblin heart. I had a job to keep cool when I was near her; to speak to her, whenever I did so, as a man might speak to the moon. I felt her so absent and icy. But it took a mere nothing, a shifting of eye or of limb, and I felt her presence nudging my hip again, a tinderbox, a smouldering fire of the flesh huddled against me. A throwback, I suppose, to abduction-night, and the journey back with her head on my shoulder, a voluptuousness I never ceased to savour, inch by inch and ounce by ounce, with eyes, ears, nose and fingertips, until every emanation of her, be it lilt of voice or bloom of cheek, was there in my veins injected and absorbed. And thus like a spirit summoned to a séance, from disembodied idol she was turning into palpable ectoplasm, an imperious sparkle in the darkness.

The odd thing is, though, that the heightened governance she wielded over my heart did not seem challenged in the least by this recent Cecilia, who seemed born from a rib of her rival, propagated by layering or gemmation, the two of them bound fast together and growing like Siamese twins – a pair who, given fresh matter, might proliferate ad infinitum . . . Love? Was this, then, love? A hydra with two, three, a dozen heads? I moved to the window seeking an answer, head bent over midnight in the Corso, elbows pressed to the cool slab of the sill. Yes, love was this: Venera, Cecilia, and any other tender-limbed creature, soft to the touch, and cavilling, and inexplicable as music; for what music says to us we do not know, though it fills us as a pail fills up with milk. Venera, Cecilia, Isolina . . . All at once they became as but a single image of my desire, a sole phantom of roseate flesh that exactly filled the empty space in the circle of my arms . . .

Isolina's window on the house across the way was in darkness, but it seemed in that dark to be fragrant with her sleep, and to cradle her affectionately, as a sugared almond nestles in a bonbonnière. I was waiting, before going to bed, for the nightly round of the barber's-shop quartet, due at any moment. With professional impartiality, no questions asked, they treated each sleeping beauty to the same serenade of sighs. Bigamist, trigamist, polygamist: such was I, even as they were. Multifariously and without distinction in love with the sex. Not sufficiently so, perhaps, with Madama Amalia, upon whom I was more rarely and carelessly incumbent of a night, capable even of whispering first one name and then another into her hair. She showed no sign of resentment. Except that one morning, when she came to call me, this was the speech she made while still in her lilac nightie.

"Professore, we must come to an understanding. I see you getting thinner, becoming a mere sprat, as bony as a kitchen crucifix. I don't blame myself, or the little things we get up to. These things put roses in your cheeks. My late lamented used to say that love makes 'em plump, and sorrow makes 'em hollow. He was right, too. But your trouble is, you've got a hole in your bucket! You're all at sixes and sevens, and it's time you got married."

"That makes two," said I. "First Mariccia and now you."

"I'm speaking against my own interests," she went on. "I'm crazy about you, but I have to think of it from your point of view. What you need is a family. You're kind, young, and salaried. You wear glasses. Speaking for myself, you've brought me my little bit of comfort. Where could I find a better son-in-law? . . ."

Son-in-law? God Almighty! I clapped a hand over her mouth, breaking off negotiations, and fled to school for the end-of-term farewells. These, an occasion for frolics and flowers, soon turned into a carnival in miniature, such was the scope for licence and forbidden intimacies. Dumping their school overalls in the cloakroom, the girls besieged the teacher's desk in a laughing, multi-coloured mob. With a pang of regret I disengaged myself, made my way reluctantly to the door. So then, the school year is over. Bang goes another slice of youth.

Here I am standing on the pavement outside the Caffè Orientale, sipping interminably at a glass of *granita*. Buridan's ass, havering between two banquets. In Upper Módica Maria Venera awaits me, the *Anabasis* open on the table under the orange-shaded lamp. The page for translation: Clearcus encamps beside a great garden, *engùs paradèisu megàlu* . . .

But here on the pavement, here as I stand, who should pass by but Antonio, Don Nitto's chauffeur, and he tells me I am wanted up at the mansion, to look over a basketful of antique shards unearthed by Nitto's tenants up near Monte Tabbuto. It occurs to me at once that I shall see Cecilia, get to meet her . . . Caught between this paradise and that, between two Edens, what to do?

Bless me if just then, waving farewell to girl-friends, flushed and flippant, eyes playing hide-and-seek beneath a black mop of hair, Isolina didn't whip by. She seemed not to notice me, flattened as I was against the wall to let her pass. All the same, no sooner was she by than her ringing laugh gave me the hint of a false note held a fraction too long, as if she was bursting to tell the world in general, and me in particular, that she was alive-alive-O, and wanted us all to envy her.

It's touch and go – shall I follow her? Stop her in the street? The anonymous letter is in my pocket. Venera handed it to me the day before yesterday without batting an eyelid, as one hands someone a dropped comb or a handkerchief. Poker-faced, as if she hadn't read it. And with a poker face I took it back.

So I have this letter. Maybe it's hers, Isolina's . . . Touch and go I follow her, stop her: "Is this letter yours? I found it on the ground just after you passed. Did you drop it?" Imagine the blushes, the swoonings! If she denies it at least I can beat a retreat saying "I thought . . . I saw it lying there . . . Well, if it's not yours I'll hang on to it . . ."

Too late! Isolina is already out of sight around the corner. Pity, though . . .

"Shall we be off then?" It's Antonio, back again in a jiffy. The roll of the dice has chosen Cecilia.

TEN

Trip to Donnalucata.
Jack-light fishing and night of love.

Don Nitto's mansion had been built on the grand scale. The drive, sloping gracefully upwards, and lined with shrubs and pines, was broad enough for three cars abreast, and the pond embraced by the twin flights of steps must have seemed an ocean to the solitary gosling swimming on it. It was a nineteenth-century building, with all the commodities of those days, including the "sirocco house", a pavilion with cyclopean walls designed to withstand the ferocity of the dog-days. Here I found Don Nitto waiting for me, dressed to the nines in white, but seated in rustic fashion on a bench, facing a pile of potsherds grimy with mud and time, and apparently poor stuff. And yet, rubbed with a fingertip, the belly of an amphora revealed a profile, the crescent of a woman's face, black against the red-brown background, and perhaps a goddess.

I looked up. "Persephone," I hazarded, if only to say something to justify this consultation. But Don Nitto, suavely addressing someone over my shoulder: "Ah, nice to see you up and doing."

I turned, and there was Cecilia, advancing calmly towards us, clad in what more or less amounted to a silk handkerchief. He introduced me, as if we were in a drawing-room. We regarded each other, she with mild curiosity, as one looks at a man wearing collar and tie on the beach; and I, having nothing to lose, with brazen amazement.

Without a shadow of doubt she was the most beautiful woman I had ever seen. Every particle of her body so perfect as to make one think it was not all nature's work, but that a skilful lapicide had here trimmed a scruple of flesh, there added another, and smoothed her breasts with pumice, and tapered her legs, and given her glance that marvellous, melancholy light, and slipped that hint of a dimple into her chin. Her every attribute was peerless, of metropolitan quality. Even the brown birthmark on her shoulder, scarcely discernible under the bronze of her tan, seemed not so much a blemish as a regal fleur-de-lys. Although, compared with the fresher charms of Venera, one thing I could all too clearly see: that hers was a perfection of ripeness, which a year or a day from now would begin to wilt. For the corners of her eyes foreboded minute wrinkles, as did her forehead at the hairline, there in the bright sunlight. The same with her gait, which at each step required an imperceptible thrust of the hips; and the flash of adult, ironical acerbity with which her lips parted as she bent to offer her mouth to Don Nitto's kiss.

The sound of her voice, when she spoke, was violet in colour.

She was got up like this to go to the sea, she said firmly. To have a swim before her imminent departure. I then remembered what they said about Don Nitto and his kept women – the biannual changing of the guard in July and January. And I looked with compassion at the woman, thinking what a deal of unhappiness she must have stacked up in the course of her life, if she had agreed to bind herself to such a stingy contract. With every luxury, maybe, but stingy. To the point of not allowing leave of absence until the last few days of internment, when Don Nitto suddenly relaxed his jealous severity, perhaps in order to draw breath before transferring it to his next bed-tenant. Odd bird, Don Nitto! For, while insisting on keeping his girls behind bars, he was the first to organize social festivities, not so much to enjoy them in person as to relish the power of election which this duty bestowed on him; the which, together with the pastimes of gambling and women, constituted the rather bizarre pleasures of his life.

"Why don't we go to the sea too?" I blurted out bravely enough, blushing at once to a record shade of crimson, then blanching to a schoolboy pallor. But, "You two go," said Don Nitto; and, addressing me: "I bequeath her to you, she's all yours, professore."

As I no-noed, and Cecilia stiffened, he continued as if to himself: "What's it matter? I can't consider myself betrayed by a woman in my pay. And I've always paid, always. I've never had anyone for love."

He sighed. Then, looking intently into empty space: "They were good times those, when I came in from the country by bike to go to the brothel, pedalling along in the moonlight. Afterwards I used to eat the melons along the roadside, pee against the wall of the roadmen's hut. It was a bit of all right, being young."

Antonio, a kind of athletic illiterate, climbed obediently behind the wheel. We set off for Donnalucata and the sea. Cecilia and I shared the back seat, though in silence. For her part, Don Nitto's words seemed hardly to have grazed her. They had left on her lips an expression of vexed indifference; offended, yes, but I could scarcely flatter myself that I was the offender, or the cause of offence. For myself, one half of me felt nauseated, while the other nourished unkind thoughts towards her, to the extent of suspecting that her expression was a fake. Frankly, if she lived with a millionaire for money, she need make no bones about having an unpaid holiday with a penniless young man for a day of seaside and idleness.

She hadn't changed her costume much for the journey; it was still just clogs and nothing. She had simply flung on a skimpy wrap to use as a bathing towel, and brought along a bag of beach junk and cosmetics, which she wedged like a rock between her body and mine, so that it pressed against my hip and gave me an excuse for breaking the ice. Why didn't we put it on the floor, I said. *I* wouldn't take advantage of the proximity; *I* took as much notice of Don Nitto's invitation as such a coarse jest deserved.

"You can tell that to your schoolgirls, professore," she retorted, though not unkindly. She remained somewhat aloof though, asking me questions about myself, about my life, and what I thought of her. I told her the truth, and she said nothing. After a while: "Life is a difficult bit of homework, professore."

Eventually, quietly, "I'll be forty soon." She seemed upset. But a moment later she was laughing. "I want to have a swim and wash it all off. Wash off Don Nitto. Don Nitto, and Módica, and you, the lot of you – and him too." She stabbed a finger at the chauffeur's back. Antonio, who was watching us in the rear mirror, muttered something between his teeth. I said, "That's O.K. by me," and took her by the hand, at the same time slipping off the curious, valuable amulet she wore on her wrist, to get a better look at it. My query about it was answered with a random fib that I don't remember.

She hardly stayed on the beach at all, she was always plunging back into the sea. I sat waiting for her under an abandoned beach umbrella, loath to get caked with salt, to follow her, dough-white as I was, into the hurly-burly of bodies and swashings. As she stepped from the water the setting sun cloaked her in a golden aureole, and for an instant she might have been a goddess of the ancient race, crowned with refulgent sunbeams.

"Persephone, I'm over here," I shouted at the top of my voice, causing a dozen female bathing-caps to swivel enquiringly in my direction. But she paid no heed. She had bent down, placid and beautiful, to inspect a drop of blood wrought upon her big toe by a rock.

When Antonio came urging us to start back I plucked up courage and told him to hop it. We were going out with the jack-lamps tonight to watch the fishing. "Come and fetch us tomorrow evening. It'll be all right with the boss."

So said I, confident of Nitto's endorsement, seeing that he was so keen on betrayals, provided he could give them his blessing in advance, from his position of well-fed minotaur.

Anyway, I really enjoyed this trip. I'd taken it several times, for the price of a tip to the skipper in cigarettes and booze. And the evening looked set fair for a dead-calm sea beneath the most propitious of all possible skies – not a glimmer of moonlight. The opposite, that is, of what the tourist hopes for, but the best conditions for a good haul.

A night to remember. We lay on the deck in the dark, peering ahead and watching, down there at water-level, the comings and goings of the outrider rowing-boat, mazes of wakes in amongst the skein of nets; or else we divined its movements from the tiny acetylene moon hung over the side, scooping up our hearts into its scuttle of yellow light.

She began to feel cold, and wrapped herself in a big sailor's blanket. I soon felt chilly myself, and asked her to share it with me. The skipper padded back and forth, ignoring us completely. Cecilia smoked away in silence, watching the fish rise, a bubbly assembly of sardines and anchovies, mackerel and skate . . . For a moment they reconnoitred the light, the boat, then settled, then surfaced again.

And now the water started to breathe, slowly. How long and how slow was the breath of the vasty sea. With that sombre thick blood of his, all around our mote of a boat, our crew of bustling mannikins, our presumptuous thought. Whereas *he* was not thinking, nor does he ever think. He only rises and falls, world without end, as the spirit moves him. The sombre, precipitous sea beneath the hump-backed cabin of the sky.

This I murmured to Cecilia to impress her with my eloquence, through lips gauchely nuzzling her hair to seek out her ear. And the night in the meanwhile strewed itself about us, a shower of black petals, inexhaustible flower. Very soon the smell of the fresh-caught fish still flicking around our feet was mingled with the odour of fish a-roasting. The deckhands were cooking their dinner, culled from their travel and their travail, as once in forest and desert did the pilgrim of the wilderness. We ate with them, and drank, and I felt groggy and happy – a convalescent.

So then I began to tell her the story of Isola Giulia, alias Ferdinandea, an islet which emerged from these waters between Sciacca and Pantellería a century or more ago. Fine, black, heavy sand, with a knoll in the middle and a little lake of boiling water on the level foreshore. The sea ringed it about, a sky-blue sea, but unctuous like oil. The island survived a while, then the sea reclaimed it. One day it will re-emerge.

The skipper overheard, and laughed. "One of these days we'll haul it up with the catch, along with the mackerel and mullet." Then he gave the word for a half-hour's breather. The men all dossed down in the stern for forty winks. Only the light of the outrider still moved along the channels between the nets. And I turned to Cecilia: "Giulia!" I called her. "Alias Ferdinandea!" And she smiled, she squeezed my hand.

When sleep overtook her, I didn't notice. I talked on, chanting my professional lullaby, until her closed eyes gave me pause, and I leant over her sleep in the likeness of a tender sentinel.

So there she is, sleeping, wrapped in a blanket on the deck. Bosom rising and falling to an uneven cadence, breath coming in a rush at first, then a long silence, a kind of death. What, is she dead? But her breathing returns, placated, bourdon music, the level sound of wind in the spring grass. Ah then she lives, she lives! Invincible in the hidden currents of her blood, alive, integral in her body, from the loop of black hair pinned at the nape to the pink-varnished tips of her toes. Alive yes, but where is she now? Where is sleep taking her off to? Her profile like the goddess of the exhumed amphora, Persephone or what you will. She too, like her namesake, coursing through the world, leaping like a wild thing, though subterranean tremors weaken her knees, and the god's lips burn on her neck. Persephone, why not indeed? Poor childeen ever on the wing, her forty years all bruised and beautiful, with the scent of a lost soul, with the selfsame tensing knot of astonished pleasure within her, the same perverse delight in yielding, in giving herself . . . Oh where are the girdles, the garlands lost in the underbrush? Loosened are the combs that curbed her hair. A single stem still clasped in her hand, the stem of an asphodel. But already the ravens are shrieking ill-omen over the heads of her handmaidens. They scatter hither and thither, and yet the maid their mistress turns not back. Maiden Persephone, where are you fleeing to? What time-worn ford are you treading beneath cold heels? What stream now steals you away? In the dark arising from this pit of sea nothing shines for me but your sleeping face in the arms of the bearded god: Hecate the golden, luciferous vision . . .

So then, my barcarole was sung and said, but she did not hear me from out of her peasant sleep. Other echoes she heard: hunting horns on the banks of Adda or Olona, out of a distant childhood, among jubilations of cockcrow and poplar, in low-lands patterned with far less inky torrents . . .

So I drew my body close to hers and clung there, between us nothing but the pliant folds of her robe. She murmured in her sleep, she vaguely stirred to my kiss. Softy I unravelled her from her cocoon. The night was deep and all were sleeping.

Were they really asleep? Was it a sham? And what about her?

"Are you asleep?" I asked. "Sleep! Sleep!" I commanded. And like a warm serpent I crept into her, I shuddered out love, I showered love into her. She didn't open her eyes, she didn't move. She wanted to mistake me for a dream and she succeeded.

At dawn, while the noisy deckhands were disentangling their nets, her first gesture was to fling up her arms and shield her eyes with her hands, as if to screen from the horrors of daylight all that she had plundered from the night. When she did look at me, she truly seemed a stranger returned from Erebus, emerged from Cimmerian depths, astonished to be alive. An emissary from unknown regions, seeming still to be harkening to the deep-sea depths. Persephone, or Isola Giulia: thus, in my thoughts, and by no other name, now and for ever would I call Cecilia.

Of all this she knew nothing. The make-believe held good only for me. She washed in sea-water and strolled among the drying nets, picking up boxes of fish and assessing weights like a fishwife, tonelessly humming the latest hits: *Arriverderci dunque, Amado mio*. I felt like a god with two left thumbs; I said to the morning "Good morning", and smiled with approbation upon my lapses.

Until the sun topped the horizon, crisping the waves with

foam and chips of gold. Low clouds moved to meet it; filmy and swift they enfolded it, great, white, riddled bandages through which it bled.

Everyone could see by now that she and I wanted to love one another, were blind and dumb with longing, and didn't know which way to turn. The deckhands began to laugh, sheepishly at first but then outright, in all innocence. Eventually the skipper rigged up a piece of sail to hide us, laughed and said, "*Orbu nun vidi, surdu nun senti*," what the eye doesn't see . . . and went back to stowing fish into boxes.

ELEVEN

Happy days in the city and on the sands. Maternal scruples of an infanticide. Farewell to Cecilia. Midnight tussle, Iacca vs. Madama.

Her replacement having arrived at La Sorda, in the person of a Calabrian lady from Longobucco, Cecilia agreed to stay on for another week, in a hotel in Módica, and have a bit of a holiday with me. A holiday which she threw herself into with childlike glee, not denying herself the whim, on meeting Don Nitto one evening outside the Conservative Club, of coolly blowing cigarette smoke smack in his face. Thus descending somewhat from her pinnacle of glory, but rendering herself, if possible, even more human and dear to me.

Darling Cecilia! What dulcet nights we spent together! Afternoons, I should say, though they seemed nights, with the shuttered windows, the sluggish light from shaded lamps on bedside tables. A room in the Hotel Trinacria, where she and I went together on our return from the sea.

Cecilia was really and truly a lovable person, and not all the drubbings of the years had managed to strip her of the film of innocence that protected her, as the rind protects a fruit, and mingled in all her doings with an air of gentle melancholy. She had a docile nature too, and accepted heart and soul the nimbus of celestial myth with which from the first I had garlanded her brow. She did her best to go along with me, asking me – no less – to tell her tales of Nausicaas and Circes, or pressing me to read her my own stuff.

Love-making was more in her line, the little skills of pleasure, into which she put a kind of diffident commitment, sweetly instructional, a touching grace.

I took pride in showing her off, I must confess, and brought her to the sea every day. At the same time I did not fail in my visits to the palazzo every evening, to administer to Venera, in lightning epitomes, my personal version of Italian literature. Seated shoulder to shoulder with the attentive girl, at the great casement flung wide on account of the heat, with my brown, bare arm still burning from the sun brushing her bare, cool, white one, I would shake the defunct poets one by one out of their lethargy, chanting their lyrics to the night like airs from Bellini. Or else, hoping to catch her fancy, rolling them off my tongue with a detachment which I considered sublime . . .

My pupil was not much taken with these solos of mine. She was too aloof by half, full of false solicitude, capable, if I arrived late, with the flush of pleasure still glowing on my cheek, of needling me with over-politenesses: I could stop coming to give lessons if I liked, seeing that I was *so* short of time these days, and had *so* much on my mind.

"What's on my mind?" I remonstrated, although everyone had seen me around with Cecilia, both in Módica and at the sea. "Something on my mind? Short of *time*?" I said with mild pique, spitefully hoping she wouldn't take me at my word.

In point of fact my time was very short. The mornings melted away between my fingers, and it was midday before I could look round. And then, the heat! Módica stank of singed flesh, of scorched tyres; it had been invaded by swarms of winged cock-roaches which milled about between houses sandblasted by the wind. The only escape was to rush to the sea. Enough to approach the coast, even before the skyline emerged from the canebrakes, and we felt the air turn to liquid around us, to a clear, permeable vessel of water, a swaying hammock of water and light the colour of lapis-lazuli.

Along the road we passed cars and carts heading inland. The drivers gave us the usual "all clear" sign, signifying that there was no police trap round the corner. Cecilia didn't understand these conspiracies between complete strangers to frustrate the law.

"You Sicilians are mad," she said, and I agreed with her.

"That's true," I told her, "but there's method in our madness. One of these days I'll tell you what it is . . ."

But here are the blue-green waves where, amid cork-floats and buoys, the most patched-up old hulk caracoles as bravely as the eight-oared gondola of the Doge himself. Here on the bibulous yellow sand throngs the half-naked holiday mob, a tapestry of red and green bathing-suits. And among it all the only splash of black is the donkey with the lemonades, pilgrim from hut to hut. On the cart behind him, white ingots of ice swathed in straw and beaded with moisture like caciocavallo cheeses.

We would get to the sea very early, Cecilia and I, as we liked to gad around a bit. In Iacca's car, grudgingly lent, or more often by bike, and all over dust from head to foot, we would make a leisurely tour of the coast, from Mazzarelli to the Aguglie, stopping wherever things were most boisterous and crowded. Such was the urge we both felt to share with kindred bodies the ceremony and pageant of our beatitude.

After our night spent out with the jack-lamps we ventured no more on the high seas. There was warfare between the licensed fishermen and the poachers, the latter armed with underwater lights and explosives. At Brúscoli they had come to blows. Risky to repeat our adventure. Small matter; it was just as much fun to be picture-postcard bathers, with a borrowed beach-umbrella to stick in the sand in the same place every day – the hole was still there; with bat and ball games and swimming races to the big rock in the distance; with furtive kisses, sandy mouth to sandy mouth, provoking pandemonium in our punch-drunk senses. Weary at length, we wended our way home, the last spark of bodily exuberance spent, blissfully sated with the day, having eaten and drunk it all up, wasting not a crumb or a drop of it.

The first Sunday in July the girls from my class at school came down to the beach. Exams had already begun, and they wanted to take their minds off 'em. They made no bones about clustering round me, amorous, garrulous, scandalized, and coy. While at my side Cecilia – Doric the legs, the head Corinthian – benevolently offered to their breathless attention the prodigy of her naked flesh, the oriflamme of our belonging. Oh, then I felt like a golden pheasant, a cock-bird crested and mine own idolater. And such I must have seemed to all around, if Iaccarino, who had escorted Madama down to the beach, came to enjoy the spectacle at close range and, draped in a caftan that gave him the air of a caravaneer, to mar my apotheosis with impertinent guffaws. Madama, nose in air, had seated herself farther off, under an awning with some girl-friends of hers. For days she hadn't spoken to me, she and the philosopher confining themselves to deploring my criminal absences, the pair of them bereft of my company and resenting it. From a distance I waved her a vague, useless greeting, which crossed wires with another greeting, addressed to me by a spindly, off-white Triton emerging from the waters in my neighbourhood, in whom with some effort I recognized Scillieri, the ex-M.P.

"See you soon, professore!" he cried, unaccountably. And, spraying me liberally with the briny, disappeared, leaving me with the uncomfortable feeling that this bonhomie might be leading up to something . . .

Later, on our feet in the beach-hut, I made tempestuous love to Cecilia, hugging in my arms the music of her, that cage of bone and blood and muscle where her melody was made, that was her masterpiece. A compact tabernacle of flesh, but also a hyacinth, a dark-hued emerald. With that dilated spider-bite in the groin, nip in the night-time from a gold tarantula.

July the Fifth, the Sixth, the Seventh . . . In search of those days I turn to a stack of old newspapers, I caress the yellowed pages. The headlines speak of the bandit Pisciotta in gaol at Viterbo, of Mr Kinley, the Wizard of the Flames, putting out the fire at Oilwell No. 9, at Ragusa, and having his picture taken dressed as a salamander. Well and good, but the white heats of my heart, who will fan them, who will extinguish them? The papers speak of wars and of treaties, of births and deaths. They never mention Cecilia and me, although, as long as I live, her unrivalled body against mine, upon my body the stirring vigour of hers . . . these things I will not forget . . .

As long as I live, I say: the sole, dismayed custodian of herself and me, of those shared moments that today are nothing . . . I am always dismayed when I think of the immeasurable cemetery of minutes, each one resembling the swelling of a wave, the bellying of the deep-sea waters. Dying, born again, leaving no trace. It's at times like these that I remember my father.

"I feel down in the dumps," he would sometimes say of a morning.

"Why's that?" I'd ask.

"No particular reason," he would answer, and then, on second thoughts: "It's memories. Last night was one long film-show."

He was thinking of the film-show of memories, fought all night long in sleep. He said exactly that – "fought", for in our dialect we "fight" not only people, but things, events, the slings and arrows of the daily news and of history. So true it is that for us, in Sicily, every least act in life is a gruelling hand to hand, a mortal risk, a struggle to the death. So what can I say, I, my father's son, if I am for ever fighting memories, their lies, their tricks, their red herrings . . . For ever going forth to battle but always falling, bleeding and falling, bleeding and fighting . . . A spectre roams the roads of Sicily, and it is my youth. May I be forgiven the ambushes I have set for it, almost always bungled in any case, as befits a pipe-dreamer, a fanfaroon . . .

July the Eighth, the Ninth, the Tenth . . . The sirocco instead of winged cockroaches now brought us huge bluebottles to thud against the window-panes. In the heat of the sun the town grew as incandescent as the bull of Phalaris; many an iced drink was needed to strike pity into summer, her cannons, her javelins of vermilion flame. Before leaving for the sea Cecilia, who had repudiated Coca Cola, stopped off every time at the Pasticceria

Rizza, where she sucked an iced elixir through a straw, her face a picture of almost indecent delight.

I waited for her outside, in the Piazza dei Mercedari, witness to the rolling up of the earliest shutters, and gazing up at the bony whiteness of Monserrato, like the brow of a man deep in thought. And for a moment I would feel cleansed of the vulgarity which is the basic endowment of my nature. Unsullied within my cubic metre of air, made in the image of the town I loved, with the same tendernesses, the same rough edges, the same roaring spate in the gorges of the Lavinaro, the same swallows in my hair.

I explained this to Venera, one evening when I felt my heart brimming with love for her, for Módica, for the whole wide world. I told her that I had her home town in my very bones, and what a kinship I felt for it; how I loved her for the town's sake, and the town for her sake, and that they were all of a oneness.

"And Cecilia?" she laughed, closing the book we were reading. "Is she a town too? You certainly love a few towns, you do! An *atlas* full of 'em!"

She said this quite carelessly, and it was plain that my love-affairs amused her; they didn't touch her at all.

Nevertheless, that evening she showed me a secret. At first I thought it a brazen gesture, but then I persuaded myself it was a pious rite.

"Look," she said, going to a deep drawer and gingerly taking out a bundle. This she unwrapped. It contained a cloth steeped in blood, clotted and dried.

"My child," she said solemnly, scarcely able to restrain her tears, and leaving me speechless in the face of such belated remorse. A lone rat suddenly darting between her feet made her lose the thread, but did not shock her. Living in that ramshackle ruin had rendered her immune. I tried unavailingly to hit it with the fire-tongs, but it went to ground beneath the massive bulk of the walnut sideboard.

*

July the Eleventh . . . Cecilia had to leave, to go back north. For the last time I begged the loan of the car; I wanted to go with her as far as Catania. At the station, just like in Russian movies, her face was enveloped in steam. Through it I called out to her, "Farewell fairy queen, my goddess. Farewell Persephone! Farewell Isola Giulia!"

I was echoed by her violet-coloured voice, already distant: "Alias Ferdinandea!"

I had told Iacca I'd be back the following day, the idea being to persuade Cecilia to put off her departure for twenty-four hours, to concede me another night. It wasn't on, and I travelled the road home slowly, honking the horn every so often to keep myself company. I drove without haste, thinking about my love-affairs, maintaining that they were infatuations not so much with a woman as with myself, and that they could be many and various and contemporaneous simply because in each I loved only myself. One has to fall in love with oneself, I mused, before falling in love with someone else. So that now I would naturally return to Venera, to love myself in her. I would, like a lion-tamer, whistle up my heart from its holiday and shut it up in its former cage – Venera and the town.

In the meantime I passed fields and villages, and dancing before my eyes were lamps and stars. If it was not the moon and her morphine, then it had to be a veil of sleep distorting my vision . . . I felt good though, and glad to be getting back between my fond, familiar sheets, even if I had no wish to speak to anyone at home, and sincerely hoped that Iacca and Madama had already retired to their respective rooms, she to talk in her sleep, he stentoriously to snore.

As soon as I arrived, to be on the safe side I slipped off my shoes just inside the street door, and crept upstairs with furtive tread. A superfluous precaution, as I soon realized: neither of them would have noticed the noise of my return in any case; for in passing my landlady's door I was arrested by a mewing sound which was clearly not that of Quo Vadis?, but the voluptuous arpeggios I knew of old. This being so, it would have been a waste of time to knock at Iaccarino's door; I already knew that his bed was intact, and that, given a little patience, I would shortly see him in his hirsute nudity flitting along the passage.

I approach Madama's door which, in line with her usual habits of trust and negligence, is scarcely pushed to. I only have to touch it, and it collapses like a house of cards. I enter, flick on the light, and what the devil! . . . The spectacle offered is faithful to the script, though with one variant. In view of the fact that the philosopher is not, so to speak, performing normal administrative functions but, bareback upon the martyr and accomplice ewe, ramlike he strives; and with so much acrobatic zeal as at first to be unaware of my presence. For an instant I am uncertain whether to cough, kick up a rumpus, creep away on tiptoe, or unseat the rampant beast with my bare hands . . . They untangle themselves, hysterical, yelling the while, and we start elbowing each other about, all three of us, while a bubble of laughter swells and balloons inside us into an enormous belly-laugh, long, unbridled, without a drop of bitters in it, that roars through the open door to the remotest bed-chambers of the building, disturbing their conjugal apathies and, from the porter's peephole to the actuary's attic, blazes away in those awakened ears not otherwise than, each 24th of May, does the fanfare of the Bersaglieri shatter the Imperial Forums.

FOURTH ASIDE

Interlude of laughs and yawns.

What an uncouth shift of tone, don't you think, dear reader? What a soulless crescendo! I bet you didn't like it. I don't like it myself. But listen, reader, I'm not making the least effort to please you, or myself either. You have to understand that my devouring passion is boredom, that I'm never happier than when I'm being trying, and dying of boredom. Shall I put my cards on the table? Too long have I spent encircling my heart with a barbed-wire entanglement, vulcanizing it, biodegrading it; too long reading my past in Carbon-14, the future in coffee-grounds, the present in Rorschach tests . . . Ending up every time with a sentence signed by persons unknown, a Joseph K the Second, KO'd by hooded judges, inquisitioned, tortured by a jury of twelve blind men and true . . .

Do I digress? Of course. Talk in non sequiturs? No doubt about it. The French have the term *petite mort* for the swoon one falls into after making love. Well, I write in a state of perpetual *petite mort*, with outbursts of hysterical exhilaration. And I realize I've done everything wrong from the start, that the proper angle of approach was quite another: a dossier on myself to be dropped on the sly into the box marked COMPLAINTS, as in that lament from the "underground", more or less a century ago, "I am a man alone, I am a sick man . . ." Someone got there before me. Someone always does. Even though I've a better right to sickness than he had, being, as I am, one whole metastasis from head to foot. Yet incapable of maturing into a tragic character, into a man.

If this be the case, why not attempt to save my skin with jollity? I've been promised a course of treatment. I don't know exactly what it is, but I like the name: autogenous training. However, I have an idea that it's a wee bit similar to what I'm doing now, writing a piece more in jest than in earnest, as a lying spy and a spying liar, with all the spotlights trained on me, and setting myself up as conquering hero. Rather as years ago, faced by another *nuit blanche*, I would lie on my right-hand side and picture a Pau–Luchon stage in a fantacycling Tour de France, with the topnotch hill-climbers of all time, Trueba, Bottecchia, Gaul, Bartali, Binda, Coppi, Robic, Vietto, Bahamontes . . . and me among them, thrashing them all on the last steep gradient, in the mud.

A childish compensation, it must be said, but effective enough to let me get the better of myself, and to place a nightly crown upon my head.

So – eyes on me, therapist-reader, solitary partner and adversary. Brace up and repeat after me: "What a bore, what a scream, what a fag, what killing fun!"

TWELVE

July and her pastimes.
A ramble among the ancient grottoes.

Thus passed July. Each day a spark of fire, all thirty-one a burning bush. Liquid tongues flickered within me, licked through my veins. Leaving the house I tottered like a drunkard; incited by the sun I burned, and thought myself immortal.

My family wrote from home. Why didn't I come back? I said I was staying on for a while yet, to see my pupils through their exams. That, at least, was the excuse. The truth was that this new town had got under my skin; I floated in the luminosities of her eyes, I slumbered in the cradle of her hands. What more can I say? I owned every street, on those scorching afternoons when I alone, alone with Iaccarino, trod the honey-coloured pavements. Each ribbon of sky, framed by the corniced roofs, belonged to me by right of usufruct.

The days sped by. In the mornings I would pop in to the school, mingle with the ganglions of waiting candidates, give advice, reassure them before the exam. They were quaking; their eyes grew wide in apprehension at the pot-luck of the questions: "Hey, come off it! A *third* Romantic Period?"

On one of these occasions Isolina came up to me, with a smell of cake about her and, stuck to her lip, a blob of custard cream that wobbled as she spoke.

"What's he like, this head examiner?" she asked detachedly, addressing the air rather than me, though I was her sole audience. But she seemed so much the little girl, with those paste earrings, and the pert red bow in her hair, and the fringe combed into separate strands on her forehead; so withdrawn and unfathomable in the closet of her body that I didn't even answer, but merely blew lightly at her mouth, so that the scrap of cake fell off. She shot me a look of fury, eyes aflash like Mafia daggers, wanting to shriek me God knows what, but her voice stuck in her throat. It was Licausi, materializing like magic at her side, who bore her off. They disappeared . . .

Next, accompanied by Alvise, here's Maria Venera. Not involved in this session herself but anxious to take stock and get the atmosphere, what with her own exams coming up in October. Perhaps the first time she's been out since the night of the abduction, for she looks positively blanched amid so much of the bare and bronzed. The young teachers flock round her like a mob of suitors, embark on a dance of bees around the flower of her. They press her with questions: will she come dancing, at least, at the great mid-August Gala?

She said nothing. With her eyes she delegated the answer to her grandfather, but he hemmed and hawed; the question had nettled him. Finally he muttered "We'll see, we'll see," bewildered by the feminine bustle, the flutterings, chatterings, gigglings, the ripplings of amorous limbs. The hubbub reached all the way to the entrance-hall and caressed his senses as, in his heyday, had the rustlings of chorus-girls in the wings of some transalpine cabaret.

When they left, I walked with them a little way, the old man in the middle, I to starboard, she to port; and I stole sidelong glances at her as best I could, making do with the only visible protrusion – within their restraining black bodice, the tips of her breasts. But instinctively I checked myself when, raising my head to the salvo of the midday bells, I sensed that a dapper little figure was eyeing us from his balcony; the dapper little figure of Liborio Galfo . . .

Lots of good talk about sport and books, in the evenings spent beneath the quatrain of palm-trees in the Narrows; many a twilight altercation over Socialism in the back rooms of bars or semi-shuttered pharmacies. The expanse of the sky spread over the valley like a massive counterpane, and the gullies of empty hours filled up with words. I'd shout as loud as the rest of them, thumping my fist on the table and dissevering good from evil with the slash of an axe. And I quarrelled with Iaccarino who, rightly or wrongly, simply didn't believe in pardon on this Devil's-Island Earth, and refused, as he was wont to say, to flirt with ghosts while waiting for the next Greek Calends . . . When I crossed him by rooting for Utopia, which included Venera and my designs upon her, Iaccarino scolded me thus: "Bottom marks in politics, sub-zero in love." And he added, "You're paying the usual price for love. Do you think you can indulge in it scot free?"

I came back with a "Look who's talking!" but without pressing the point, for fear he might shove Madama back in my bed . . .

The dancing parties were starting up at La Sorda, at one mansion after another: Villa Tasca, Villa De Leva, Villa Salmè . . . With a moon waxing little by little from slender to obese, and in colour from languid water-lily to rubicund doubloon . . .

By courtesy of Don Nitto I was always on the guest-list. Before handing me an invitation he would ask solicitously after Cecilia, anxious to know if I'd found her satisfactory. He even went so far as to make me a present of the antique red and black vase as a memento of her. It would still be in my possession had not Quo Vadis?, egged on by I know not whom, played cat and mouse with it one morning, scattering the fragments to the four corners of the earth.

At these dances I saw a lot of Trubia. We asked the same girls to dance, vied for precedence on the most sought after dance-cards. I recall hepped-up, outlandish nights, with smoochy music and us trotting blithely around the dance-floors, amid flowerbeds and pools and tables laden with drinks. Each and every one of us positive of being in bliss, in a seventh heaven of bliss, all of us at a never-again zenith of youth, boys and girls together, with our supple limbs, our flushed cheeks, the spark and triumph of our eyes, gods and goddesses all, despite our off-the-peg poplin suits, our long silk evening dresses, our routine platitudes.

"May I have the honour of this dance?"

"Do you happen to know the name of this tune?"

"Let's have a whisky at the bar."

And at dawn we all trooped off to the "Sorcio" for a plate of spaghetti as soon as the place was open; we waited for the sun before going to bed . . .

Venera was never there at these dances, and I wasn't sorry. I preferred to see her at home for our lessons. After Cecilia left I never skipped a visit; content, for lack of better, to get a good look at her every day, rather as a fanatic, day after day, will put the same record on the gramophone. Since her mild attempt at chumminess in showing me the winding-sheet she had grown wary, almost hostile; nor did she appear to remember that I was her sole accomplice, the only one abreast of her private woes. My sideslip with Cecilia had, alas, made no impression on her, and whenever I brought the thing up she listened with bland indifference. Once only, after a party in the gardens at Ragusa Ibla, did she enquire of me how the loveliest of the débutantes were dressed – the Mormina sisters, the Scichilone and D'Angelo girls . . . Who had they danced with most? She heard, without batting an eyelid, the name of her cousin Sasà.

It had not escaped my notice that she had forgone her holiday with the Aunts this summer, but I could scarcely imagine this was simply to avoid her cousin. It wasn't her style to give him the satisfaction of feeling feared and therefore shunned. More than anything else, I suppose, it was pride that kept her in town, the stubborn pride of penury, and the mortification of having always to match up, in the same, plain black dresses, to the resplendent apparel of her rivals. On top of everything, Alvise was far from well. He woke every night with palpitations, and called to her for help. She looked after him conscientiously, for she had grown up with a rush since the elopement, and toughened, and become more aware. She had given up playing sweet nothings on the keyboard, and stayed up late over her books. On one occasion she staggered me with a quotation in French, another time I saw her with a formidable anthology in hand. She was becoming a student to be reckoned with. Consequently I was all the more taken with her, seeing that I, as a teacher, had a way of dubbing bright pupils beautiful even when they weren't. So my feelings flared up again, though my manner remained unchanged: remote and touchy. Certain it was that those few days of sexual success had not been enough to put me wise, or give me a swagger. I had immediately relapsed into my habitual emotional slavishness: liable to get het up but not to let it be seen; elated and yet deluded when near her; disposed to desire but scared to possess her; resigned to being unloved, yet livid that she loved another . . . Everything in fact, dear reader, as in Chapter 1. The same ups and downs of mood, depending on whether I felt her the more or less willing to play her part in my scenario of unrequited love. She, unfettered, blasé, delectable, in the pageant of her way of walking, of talking, her every gesture and the fragrance of her, all that fashioned the memorable, unmistakable, sovereign She; myself, looking on from my box in the darkened theatre, gnawing my knuckles to all eternity.

One Sunday, when Alvise was feeling a little better, he determined to come with us to Íspica, to visit the famous Cava – a long, narrow gorge riddled with ancient grottoes and rock-hewn chapels. He had bitten off more than he could chew, and began to flag at once. He took a seat on a boulder and budged no more, though he encouraged us to go on and explore further into the place. On we went then, novices in a happy, green Beyond. No clanking of chains, lamentations, tenuous flutter of bats, such as accompanies the subterraneous travels of every Aeneas or Chosen Vessel. Here, along the barren cliff-face, was a maze of tunnels and openings offered to the laughter of the light. Not a prospect, not a frescoed figure, which did not gently urge one to live life.

I grasped Venera's arm, I helped her out of narrow clefts

where she had winkled in, partly in search of some cool, so scorching was the sun, but even more from a girlish impulse to hide, to play games. There's no doubt it's difficult, when we are children, to stick at playing grown-ups for very long.

Inside the largest burial chamber there was a heavy fustiness, as in an old cellar. Sweating as we were, we shivered. We moved on in little leaps and bounds, dodging the empty niches. One of these took her fancy, a tiny one side by side with a larger one.

"A little girl and her father," I ventured.

"The child-wife of a king," she corrected me.

On we went, peering about, losing each other, linking up again, through colonnades made now by the artifice of man, now by the accidents of nature. A huge centipede tried to follow us, failed, quickly went to earth when it sensed above it a threatening boot. Venera, with breathless courage, wanted to upturn the stone.

There were voices approaching. Many voices, men and women together. For the fun of it we hid behind a pillar of tufa, waiting for them to pass. This party was not in search of tombs, we realized, but of herbs growing in the walls of the gorge. They were simple folk, chatting away pleasantly in dialect. We stood stock-still, for the game of hide-and-seek is one of the most amorous in the world, if there are two of you: two alone against the rest, more alone and amorous than naked abed together.

From our hiding-place we saw a sun-drenched strip of pathway, dazzling bright. Shadows of shapes appeared on it, wavered, passed on. Her breath was on my neck. Silence reigned again, the herb-gatherers must have reached the foot of the valley, we could hear them no more. Venera broke away from me, flustered perhaps, but smiling; and she moved towards the cave-mouth. Here, watching us, was a little girl of five or so, leaning against a rock. Not scared, just earnest-eyed. A stray, a straggler from the party, we imagined. Or else . . . Maria Venera looked at the tiny empty tomb, then at me, with laughing eyes. Taking us, I imagine, for the owners of the place, the little girl preserved her serious air. All the more so when Venera looked into her eyes and put her finger to her lips as if to suggest a secret pact. The girl did likewise, pressing her small finger firmly to her own lips, and then, walking backwards, slowly moved away.

Arm in arm by now we went in the verdant world, a Garden of the Hesperides between two prison walls. Life in death, death in life etc. This notion had no appeal for Venera, who flew lightly up a path fit for a mountain goat to a grotto pendent over the void, stepped forth laughing onto a natural rock balcony, mimed Juliet, then skipped back down.

She was wearing black, as ever. The same threadbare muslin dress fit only for the rag-and-bone man. But it became her so well, it turned her to a bird, with those long, slim legs of hers and her natural bent for flight. A stork, a crane, a heron. If not a lark, the way she sang. For now she had begun to sing; like Cecilia a songstress, but with a less trashy repertoire. "*Love is a strange bird* . . ." O yes Maria Venera, who ever will tame it?

Therefore, as she bent to gather sweet marjoram and capers, in imitation of the peasant-women just passed by, "Truly you don't want to?" I found myself saying to her bending back. "I want to marry you."

She turned in surprise, as surprised as I was myself at having thought these words and uttered them.

"What do you mean?" she asked, caught off balance. She was plainly trying to gain time, to make hurried calculations about something. "In spite of everything?"

"In spite of everything," I said.

But she had already taken to her heels. The flicker of a lizard or a viper had scared her, she told me from a distance. I didn't believe her of course. She was thinking out her answer, she had run away to think of an answer. When she came back she gave me a downright "no".

"No, I won't marry you. Galfo yes, I would have married him. He would have been a servant to me all my life. And what I need is either a man or a servant. Whereas you're neither one nor the other, really . . . What's more, you're no age in particular – not a child, not young, not old. Even though soon, very soon, you'll become all old."

I didn't answer. Maybe she was right, maybe not. How did she manage to be so sure?

"So you've got your marching orders," she said. And throwing up her arms she pulled my head down to hers, and kissed me briefly.

That was the way she was: curious perfidies, second thoughts, illogical impulses . . .

It was midday, and we rejoined Alvise in the shade of a clump of hibiscus. He was holding a flower, and pointed out the five wedges of deep colour nestling at the heart of the five red petals.

"It won't last," he told us. "In a few hours it'll close, and be just a little wrinkled bag. It doesn't last long, hibiscus."

He then tucked in with gusto to the pizzas we had brought for our picnic, and at long last gave us the full version of his tale of love, uric acids and death at Vichy, in 'Twenty-One or 'Twenty-Two, with a certain Mademoiselle Colombe or Marie-Edwige or Tiddlypush Chauvet.

FIFTH ASIDE

Umpteenth encore by the author, caught between arsis and thesis, right way on and inside out.

So I was young and happy, that summer of 'Fifty-One. Young and happy, young and . . .

What? That's not true. It's all a swank.

Dear reader, it's not that I want to leave you in the lurch. Far from it. I well realize that on this earth I'm in arrears with the rent, and nothing but prattle to pay my debts with. I also realize, it's as plain as a pikestaff, that these solfeggios of groans between one natter and the next are not helping me to get any better. But what to do? In order to describe a happy summer, wait for one to come along? Wait for this autumn to pass, this shrinking heart; for this city to pass from me? To this city I would fain have come with the tread of Brennus, to sack the place, to kick down the gates, to water my roan at the fountain in Piazza di Spagna. And instead I come incognito, a paying postulant, forever sitting in some new specialist's waiting room with a folder full of analyses on my knee. And in October too, mind you! . . . They tell us, dear reader, about the cruelties of April, but what price October? A saturnine October in league with all the worst isotherms and isobars and isoblahs of low pressure, the never-ending drip from gutters onto the oilskins of roast-chestnut vendors, the wheezing of weathercocks, the *slop-slop-slop* of the Tiber under the arches of Ponte Sisto. All of these are things to provoke a yearning, a mouth-watering, I dare not tell you for what . . . Maybe it's that I'm an omnipathic, pathic to a million things, and therefore also to meteors, airy, watery or fiery, for I am troubled not only by April but by every one of the twelve months, torrid, gelid or tepid as they may be, and by every day of the year, not excepting the leap-year supplement. Plainly I was born to live in an era devoid of seasons. Or at least, if it has to be, this rotten weather, in the century of loden coats and gaiters. How handy a pair of gaiters would come in now, as the turn-ups of my trousers flop like leaden sponges against my ankles, and I am distressed by damp in my right shoe and my left, back at past one in the morning and sounding the buzzer at the Albergo del Sole.

I wake at the Albergo del Sole, a stone's throw from Campo de' Fiori, nerves in a sudden jangle.

At first I can't find my bearings. I put out a groping hand in search of the familiar, reassuring presence of a friendly slumber at my side. And in a flash I am on the edge of the bed, in my underpants, legs dangling, divining, as if glimpsed in the throat of a chimney, a thread of light between my sewn-up eyelids; and it bids me good morning. I know where I am now, and who I am. I can account for the mouse-grey strip of almost Novembrine gloom that slipped a minute ago between the slats of the Venetian blind. And the distant roar of the first buses, and the smell of aniseed, of rotten straw, of the city as it wakens in the rain. Day is breaking, and here I sit, in this sorry semi-darkness, feeling hard done-by and calling myself softly by name. How odious it is, this Sèvres heart of mine – FRAGILE: HANDLE WITH CARE – if, as when I was a boy, all it takes is a whiff of autumn to give me a sense of permanent failure, of irremediable bankruptcy; to make me wonder what I'm doing here in this double room without bath, yesterday's socks rolled up in my shoes, a newspaper over the jerry and a tube of Gardenal on the bedside table. Alas, poor Gesualdo. Because, let's face it, I'm on the brink. I could drop in my tracks any minute and die without having understood a thing: why I have lived, and am dying, or anything at all. Without knowing even whether in this apocryphal pastiche I have been the hanged man or the hangman, whether I have played my part decently, whether the performance has been up to standard, nothing to be ashamed of. And that's the best we can say. Although I continue to wonder, in God's name, what the worst might be . . . Perhaps the atrabiliousness of being sixty, and the unavailing objections of the defence in the penultimate hearing of Universe vs. Gesualdo; or the adieus of the *jeunes filles en fleur* who look at me, if at all, as at a stick of furniture due for removal . . . Or the feeling of being a straggling *Pied Noir* with neither rifle nor *képi*, clambering up dune after dune – totally abandoned – the whiff of Arabs in the air – not a ghost of the flag! Could this be the reason? Or is it that I was robbed of my big scene, the one I wanted all to myself, in regal ermine instead of these bit-player's tatters? . . . Or is it health, just a simple matter of health? Whatever the answer, for the second time in two days, without warning, but gently enough, I attain the difficult orgasm of tears.

THIRTEEN

The Gala Ball, from ten o'clock until one in the morning.

Came the day of the Grand Open-Air Ball: a Tuesday, the mid-August holiday of Nineteen Fifty-One. At Chiaramonte Gulfi, in the garden of evergreens poised above the valley. Riding in the sky at the outset was an exhibitionist circus moon, though big clouds very soon hid it.

(Album of that evening embalmed in memory, phantom with many faces, one by one defaced with a † . . . If I knew the formula I would awaken you . . . And yet each time I don't quite manage, I miss you by a hairsbreadth, a hairsbreadth and a half . . .)

(Always the same: me on the brink of a grace that fails, a traitorous miracle. Like a tune on the brain, and you know every lilt of it, but your voice plays tricks on you . . .)

Here I am then, with a handsome head of hair, in a powder-blue suit, seated at a table with a Sasà Trubia almost unrecognizable now that he's shaved off his beard. From sheer politeness I sip at the cocktail he has bought me, and immediately splutter into my handkerchief. The night is charcoal-grey all about the shining dance-floor. I imagine how this sunken ring of light and sound, this red crater full of expectant hum, might look from the cabin of an airship: a blazing disc, seen from up there, but so minuscule, so menaced on every side by such a darkness! I rise, I lean out over the railing high above the murk of the valley. What silence! Though, when I turn, the merry-go-round of touchingly fond hopes is spinning, the ladies whirl with their beaux, they smile, they laugh, the deceased-to-be, the dear departeds of Nineteen-Ninety-Nine . . . All unaware that an unseen horde of boys and girls as yet unborn, but lurking in their loins, in their silk-swathed bellies, will soon enough have shuffled them off into the grave; unaware that the mindless horde of the future is galloping invisible behind them, with spearpoints pricking the ribs of this minute of happiness, fleeting and fruitless . . .

We were among the first to arrive, me and my two cronies. After parking the car on a slope not far from the gate, smoking nonchalantly we strolled in to show our tickets; and there, among the other helpers, was Isolina.

"I've passed! Eighty per cent average!" she plumed herself to Licausi, her eyes on me. She promised to come and dance soon, but was busy for the moment with the entrance tickets and organizing the charity competitions and lotteries planned for later in the evening. Rose-cheeked and radiant, her shapely shoulders bare beneath a chiffon stole, the hint of a shadow marking the furrow between her immature breasts . . . We enter. Along the pathways the gravel scrunches under our feet. A trumpeter is warming up with an arpeggio. It's early yet, no couples on the floor, the tables filled with the same old bachelor faces, our brazen tribe, always the first on the spot. Whereas it does not befit a young lady to appear impatient.

At this point Sasà Trubia beckons me over to his table. Just me, he wants to have a word with me alone. About Venera, I assume, and my heart misses a beat. I too would like to talk to him about her, to get it off my chest at last. However, he only wants to ask me to beg Don Nitto not to cash that cheque for the moment. Not that it would bounce, but . . . Just not to cash it for the moment. There's a certain scheme in the offing . . .

Very well, I'll plead his cause. Then I pluck up courage.

"Sasà, I'm in love with a girl who doesn't want me."

With that trumpet blasting right into his ear he scarcely grasps what I say. When he does, he starts pulling my leg about it.

"I'll put in a good word for you. Who is she?"

"Your cousin Maria Venera."

This shakes him. He can't get a word out. At this precise moment up comes Iaccarino, monster of tactlessness, planting himself before us and dancing a jig, first on one foot and then on the other, accompanied by writhings of anguish, as if from the impelling effect of raging corns or emunctory urgency. Inevitably, a chill descends on the conversation.

Meanwhile the family parties are arriving in swarms, and the dance gets under way. They play *Tico Tico*, and a jumping bean with a straight face, the petty Baron Puleo, takes the floor with Signora Virzi, our lady notary. Isolina, finished with her duties as gatekeeper, dances unceasingly, the cynosure of all eyes, looking down her nose at the necktie of her squire of the moment. Licausi, in ambush behind a shrub, never takes his eyes off her, dying for her to extricate herself and rejoin her family at their table. Thereupon he falls on her from the rear, knocking over chairs and lamps beneath the benevolent gaze of Mum and Dad, and claiming his right to preferential treatment. She seems favourably disposed, rises to her feet again, and they dance in silence.

"He's hotted up, has Licausi, after being such a wet blanket," comments Iaccarino, while surveying the proceedings, one foot on the dance-floor and the other on mine.

"There's no respect these days," agrees Sasà vaguely. Then, turning to me, in an undertone, "So Venera doesn't want you, eh?"

I nod, but get no further. Iaccarino, between one shot of booze and the next, has started on one of his numbers. Precisely as I feared, and I did so beg him not to. Not to drink, I mean, and to cut down on the talk. I alone know what it cost to wring an invitation for him out of Don Nitto. Yet here he is, with the night still in its infancy, already half-seas-over. Dead set on giving a running commentary on the party, like a herald at some bygone tournament, or a television compère.

"One, two, three, testing testing . . . there, advancing on the right we have Donna Letizia Mistretta. Following in her wake, her husband: *cornu petit ille, caveto!* From the left a clarion-call replies. It is the Gangemi–Nicita duo, cleaving the throng as the prow of a corsair xebec rives the waves. He, where his foot falls, there the grass lies withered. She is a match for him, a monument. What a toothsome dish for the starvelings on the Raft of the 'Medusa'! . . ."

"You and her," I whisper in Sasà's ear. "I know all about it. Do you love her? Do you want to marry her too?"

But Iaccarino, turning to me: "Blast you," he storms, "why aren't you laughing?"

Then, spotting a voluptuous female alone in the lamplight, "Signorina Varcadipane!" he cries. "O marvel, O mystery! O my too too lovely tulip, O you whom I might have loved, O you who will soon know it! Seated unbestirrèd in your chair, madonna sought by no one, Iaccarino will seek you out."

We were fuming, but he wouldn't leave off.

"A fake, she can only be a fake: too beauteous is she to be true. Already, fifty years hence, I hear a voice say: 'Grandma, were you a beauty in your day?' 'I was but once,' she will reply. 'One August holiday evening.'"

He rose, majestically moved across, performed a bow, and spoke at length to her large, overblown bosom, on the tremulous seas of which played the dazzle of a yellow blouse.

"Damn and blast the man!" Trubia burst out. Then, curtly to me, "Marry her? Are you trying to be funny? Cousins don't marry. Their blood doesn't mix. The children turn out peculiar . . ."

"Ah yes, the children," I said, intending a mild dig at him.

He shot me a glance of genuine bewilderment. He knew nothing, then, about the miscarried child. Venera must have kept it from him. Be that as it may, he shut up like a clam on observing, bearing down upon us, a certain myopic Byzantine empress bejewelled like the Begum. The daughter, I surmised, of Virgadauro the goldsmith.

"Not just now, not just now, dear boy," he said. "Get out there and dance. What are you waiting for?" And he packed me off, hauling me to my feet and launching me onto the dance-floor. And thus he was left alone with the lady.

Dance? Well, come to think of it, that's what I've come for. Have I so soon forgotten my resolve to make war on the world? To pair off with the first available female and shout in the face of the world, "World, you're mine!" For if Venera will not stoop, the rest of the reserve is still thick with game. Not one single quarry, but two, nay three, will the skilful hunter subdue, as did a lone one of the Horatii three Curiatii subdue.

The party was brightening up. All of a sudden the floor was crammed, and I wasn't sorry. No longer any need to do the steps. It was enough to sway together on the spot in an atmosphere of sensuous hugger-muggerdom. *Bésame, bésame mucho . . . Addormentarmi così . . .* How many shining eyes, how many credulous faces, afloat on a maelstrom of hair-oils, after-shaves, feminitudinous unguents! A many-aroma'd ambrosia coiled through the surviving interstices between body and body, and it seemed as simple to swim there as it was in his fishtank for Don Cesare's fish.

Now they were playing *Les feuilles mortes*. I didn't want to miss it, so I asked Giuliana Martoglio for the pleasure. I knew her by sight. Her face was so so, but her body was choice and sinuous as a violin, preceded by two breasts resembling volcanic cones eruptive on the highlands of Abyssinia. I was also intrigued by her habitual way of listening, smiling but silent, to anyone who tried to talk to her.

I held up the palms of my hands as if taking an oath: "You may make one last wish before dancing with me."

She smiled.

I made a bad start, colliding with a dreamy couple marking time cheek-to-cheek.

"I did that on purpose," I lied to pass it off. "I always kick the most smoochy couples. It makes them realize there's such a thing as time."

She smiled again, and it dawned on me with horror that her

smile was a lid on a void. And that as far as dancing went she was worse than I was.

"You are a Stradivarius," I lied again, "but I, alas, am no Paganini."

I need not tell you that she went on smiling. I tried a new tack.

"My first dance with any woman always thrills me. It's like arriving at the station of an unknown city."

Not even a smile this time, just a blank stare. As a forlorn hope I tried one of the tricks I kept up my sleeve.

"Come on now, tell me something about yourself: Christian name, surname, favourite flower . . . Let's see if your voice is as pretty as the rest of you."

Obediently, "Martoglio, Giuliana."

Her voice was one of holy and adenoidal innocence, so I attempted to steal from her at least a lukewarm moment.

"Abandon yourself to me like a leaf to the wind," I suggested to no avail, feeling her as stiff in my arms as a telegraph pole . . .

But the number was coming to an end, the leaves were all dead. "I return you to your bough, Miss Giuliana Martoglio," I capitulated.

Next time, when I invited Who-d'ya-ma-flip, things were both better and worse. Those were the days when couples danced in each other's arms, nattering away the while. This girl was ironical, prickly, beautiful, of a minatory beauty. Some evenings before we had danced a catastrophic Charleston. Needless to say she remembered it. How could her toes ever forget my feet?

"So we have a Past," I began.

"Too agonizing, that one. Let's invent another," she suggested brightly.

She didn't have to ask twice. I did the inventing and she played along, frequently blowing her nose with queenly grace. Rheumy and regal, her fingertips tossed me a kiss when I told her that the germs could not have chosen a lovelier nose.

Then, switching swiftly, with perfect ease, calling me *tu*:

"D'you remember the first time we met? Four years ago on the train?"

"And the kiss," I said on cue, "in the next-to-last tunnel? Do you remember it?"

"What! Not the last of all? Did I yield so soon?"

And so on and so forth until we wearied of it.

"Let's play at inventing the future instead," I suggested. But at that moment up came Michel, the French film-johnny, and tapped me on the shoulder. It was his dance. And off they sped like hart and doe together.

"Christian name, surname, favourite flower," I repeated a minute later to a tawny-haired stranger. She turned out to be Michel's photographer, and he, who gave every appearance of being on my tail, pinched her from me after a single dance. "Tónchila's love-philtre is doing its stuff," I thought as I left the floor. Not without telling Isolina in passing that she seemed to me like an Alpine lake. She flushed scarlet, and appeared to seek refuge on the bosom of Licausi, who clasped her to it.

"What's that supposed to mean?" she retorted. "That I'm all icy?"

She was anything but chuffed, and in vain I added that I would dearly love to throw a stone into that lake . . .

Hepped up, but tired out. Almost for the first time in my life I became aware of something I have since grown accustomed to: the strange flavour of non-existence in myself, in others, in the fatuous throbbing of deathlife at a certain moment and in a certain place. Just as in the valley of the grottoes every bloom and berry sprouted from nothingness. Billions – billions of billions – were the cells in us, every one of them on the march towards terminal decomposition, the ashen perfection of nothingness. Along with an inkling that the real games are played on the other side of the curtain, and that someone, himself unseen, watches us and mimes a soundless handclap. Then again, what amazed me was the sheer absurdity of it all: so many clockwork people, equipped to think, and in the world without the least reason for being there – sublimely optional. Whereas reason demanded that in their place should be nothing but the interminable vacuum of non-being . . .

What more did I need to deduce that I myself, my very own incredible me, that I, (or should I say he?) was merely a transvested non-being? I said to myself, "I dis-exist. My relations with others are nothing but a conspiracy of appearances, a mutual-aid society in which everyone stands surety for everyone else, and we all fraudulently insure each other's lives. *Videor*, *ergo non sum* . . . Or perhaps, *Sum, ergo non sum* . . ."

The person to take the mickey out of these words of wisdom, had he been present, would have been that pundit on the pre-Socratics, Professor Iaccarino. But that particular blemish, arm in arm with his tulip, had started selling tickets for the Beauty Contest. And with infernal gall he got me to buy one.

The start of the midnight fireworks. The pyrotechnist had positioned his rockets in the lower reaches of the garden, where the pathways dwindled into darkness. Everyone stopped dancing, the candles were snuffed out on the tables, then the Venetian lanterns on the low walls. A single lamp still shone among the fronds of an araucaria, then even that was doused. Darkness fell upon us, a ton of bricks. When the ring of fire was quenched on the ground, in the cabin of the airship someone raised his eyebrows . . .

The band was playing quick waltz-tunes, softly softly, while the couples in the dark, jam-packed together, were not kissing but were thinking of nothing else. . . Until the first rocket zoomed into the sky, raced and chased by a hundred others, all melting into jets and sprays of gold, shattering and reshaping note for note with the music, not so much keeping time with the band, it seemed, as conducting it.

Isolina and Licausi, inseparable, had somehow landed up beside me. Each time a rocket burst up there, and the corolla went slowly umbrellaring rosy lights, I couldn't help noticing its reflection on Isolina's throat, like a sunset glow on Carrara marble.

"You with your eighty percent in Italian!" I baited her under my breath. "Have you any idea who thought up a house slung on a string between two stars?"

She didn't know, and I in a sudden burst of daring felt for her fingers with my own. Stopping a half-inch before the touch, when I realized that around them, vast, exclusive, and hairy, was the hand of Saro Licausi.

My spirits drooped. "Cecilia," I thought. "Venera," I thought. Where were they now? The one, what echoes was she hearing, what hunting horns of Adda or Olona, at the fords of her distant girlhood? Unless, as was more likely, she was abed with some pillar of society . . .

And the other, Maria Venera, my own Carmencita of the pianoforte, what gypsy love was rocking her in her sleep? Was she sleeping? Was she dreaming?

To my speculations about Cecilia I never knew the answer. Not so, however, with Maria Venera. The instant the last boom and the music ceased together, the last flake of fire coinciding with the dying of the last note, and the lamplight blazed once more about us, reassuring the watchful eye of any vagrant aeronaut in the skies, there in the centre of the dance-floor, on the arm of Don Alvise, and clad in her mother's dress of old white Vallarmosa lace, her hair strewn loose on her shoulders, splendoured Maria Venera.

FOURTEEN

The Gala Ball, from one until three o'clock.

It was one in the morning, and the heart of the party pulsed with radiant vitality. Maria Venera had made her entrance in the dark, during the fireworks, and now that the lights were on again she seemed in one fell swoop to have gathered into her hands the hundred hearts of all the young men there; as when Don Nitto, after a banker's nine, with both his arms sweeps in the heap of winnings. Even Iaccarino, befogged as he was, appeared to be taken with her.

"Abide with us, Lady, for it is towards evening," he declaimed from his table, causing his tulip – who was also his colleague Maestra Incallina – shocked by the blasphemy of his biblical parody, to look distinctly stuffy, and finally to stalk off and leave him flat.

But I, trooping along with the rest of the young guard, tried for an age to catch Venera's eye, eventually obtaining the pittance of a distant smile. By way of compensation Alvise, who had bagged a chair near the dance-floor, lost no time in hooking my leg with his stick, demanding company. The old man seemed transfigured, full of the mettlesome spirits of yore. Perhaps it was the patent success of his grand-daughter, which led him to think that the episode of the abduction was forgotten and her honour restored with flying colours; or else it was the infectious spirit of the party, that familiar odour of make-up, liquor, and talc-strewn floor beneath the gliding heels. I was therefore obliged to remain on my feet beside him, spared at least from taking part in the "Conga", a species of dance-procession, each person with his hands on the shoulders of the person in front, winding snake-like among the trees and tables. It was only a game, but Maria Venera, who was leader, nonetheless guided the twists and turns with an air of imperious solemnity, harassing parents and chaperons even in their most secluded eyries. Until she finally led her rabble up onto the very platform, commanded the trumpet to sound the alert, grabbed the microphone and loudly gave tongue.

"Sasà Trubia!"

Ye gods! This was no joke. The night of judgement was upon us, and I confess I feared the next name on the list might be my own. A quick glance around informed me that Trubia was no longer in his seat. Earlier, in fact, when Maria Venera had first appeared, I had caught a glimpse of him among the crowd of admirers, arm in arm with the Virgadauro female, staring at the newcomer with an expression of mournful contempt, the slit of a forced smile on his lips. Turning now to seek him out, I saw he was still with the goldsmith's daughter, but otherwise deserted – the dancers were giving him a wide berth, as to a beggar, or a leper. I imagined him side by side with Maria Venera: what a handsome couple they would have made! At the moment, however, their only link was a challenge, a tragi-comic challenge where pride, revenge, desire, resentment, all the ingredients of a classic drama were blended, though in this case tainted with cheap-jack play-acting, not at all in keeping with the true sublimities of love.

"Sasà! Cousin Sasà!"

O why, O why, Maria Venera? What do you expect from him? Have you no eyes for me? Him with his dicey cheques, and ready to sell his soul to that woman and her bijouteries, don't you see? Aren't I a better bet, with my down-at-heel shoes and the new suit still to be paid for by teaching the tailor's kids their ABC? Me with my stupid nerves, like sheepdogs baying at each full moon, but so large a heart, so lyrical, such a four-poster of a heart!

Not unnaturally my entreaty did not reach Maria Venera. Stately she crowned her garments like a goddess, and before the microphone seemed a primadonna tensed for the fall of the baton. Laughing and silent for the moment, eyes on Trubia.

He moved forward, still arm in arm with the Begum. He came to the foot of the platform.

"Cousin Venera," he said. "At your service."

And she, into the microphone: "Cousin Sasà," and she laughed again. "Cousin Sasà, aren't you even going to tell your relatives. Are you going to bury the good news in your back garden?"

Then, turning to her public: "You sons and you daughters, you mammas and papas," she proclaimed in dialect. "Get ready for the wedding bells. Sasà Trubia is soon to be married."

Everyone started clapping, Trubia blanched, La Virgadauro flushed scarlet. Michel, who hadn't grasped much of this, came up to me. I was a familiar face by now.

"*Qu'est-ce que c'est que ça?*"

I didn't answer. Like the rest of the company I was on tenterhooks, divided equally between excitement, contentment, and concern. I felt called upon no longer to play the simple role of witness, but to take a conniving part in an ensemble; nor could I yet imagine for what epilogue, or what prologue.

All eyes upon him, Trubia, after a sandbagged moment, moved towards the platform, all alone. No one ever knew whether it was to confirm or to deny the announcement, or something else entirely. For halfway up the steps he met Venera coming down, and she, as she passed him, left five divine fingermarks printed on his cheek with a slap which the drummer, at the eleventh hour, tried in vain to smother with a crash of percussion. Sasà raised his hand to retaliate, brought it down towards Venera's face, and it seemed for a moment that he meant to ingentilize revenge into a caress. But the blood must have boiled in him, the caress reverted to a wallop, provoking the riposte of a glob of spittle, solemn as a verdict. All this in the space of a second, so that their two pairs of legs had no time to contradict previous instructions, but continued to carry them out to the letter, hers moving downwards, his approaching the top step. Albeit, in a twinkling called to order, precipitately the latter came scuttering down.

The heavens demanded their say, a drop or two fell from a passing cloud, we heard a lone rumble of thunder.

"Phonecall from God," said Iaccarino over my shoulder; adding, when it was clear that the rumble was to go unanswered, "Line's gone dead." He was into the third stage of squiffiness, the weepy-metaphysical, and he hung on my arm, in need of comfort.

"God," he told me, as Trubia passed us wiping his face with a handkerchief, "is too fond of blowing his own trumpet. He gives himself too big a write-up. A bit less thunder and fewer earthquakes would do him the world of good. But moderation never was his forte . . ."

Well and good, but in the chaos that reigned I had better things to do than give Iacca rope. What I wanted was to find Venera, be the first to speak to her. Hopeless: everyone had started dancing again, including herself, as if nothing had happened, as if stoking up the party would demolish all embarrassment. There remained of the episode only the shadow of an echo of a dream, the echo of those cracking slaps (or an awning flapping in the wind?), now drowned in the din of the next number. The band, in fact, were really putting their backs into it; as in the movies after a gunfight, when a black pianist bashes the keyboard at random. Around the grown-ups' tables the buzz of talk continued for longer. They had seen a boil lanced, and the skin needed time to heal over. But among the young there was no aftermath; only easy smiles of mutual understanding, the smiles of people who have an immediate, unspoken rapport. So it was I realized that everyone in Módica had known all about Venera and Sasà for quite a while. Only Don Alvise and I had been in the dark about it all.

Don Alvise . . . Yes, what had become of Don Alvise? I went to seek him out in the corner where I had left him, thinking to console him. This proved unnecessary: he hadn't noticed a thing.

The crowd on its feet had blocked his view, and his nonagenarian hardness of hearing had distorted, or robbed him entirely, of everything Venera had said, despite the microphone. In addition he was busy holding a hostage in the person of ex-M.P. Scillieri, and pouring disdain on the monocle worn by Gugliemo Giannini, leader of the Man-in-the-Street Party. He described it as the monocle of a parvenu posing as a gentleman. Scillieri didn't like this, naturally enough, but found no means of escape. I left him to his struggles and rushed off in search of Maria Venera.

No easy matter. After the incident the competition to dance with her was more furious than ever, and I never got my foot in the door. She laughed ostentatiously as she whirled about, white and proud among the lesser couples; and as she circled the floor she did not avoid, but indeed deliberately sought out, the table where Sasà was talking grimly and ten to the dozen to his presumed fiancée. The only time I saw her upset was when Galfo appeared on the scene. I didn't think he'd come; and he must have been in two minds, arriving as late as he did. He was wearing a linen suit and white shirt, a perfect fashion plate. And he plunged at once into the dance, clearing the floor around him. We saw he was wearing his professional shoes, the ones with tap-dancing toe-pieces. Everyone else stopped dancing, a ring formed around him, and the band, exclusively for him, played pre-war numbers from *Top Hat* and *Follow the Fleet*. Maria Venera was left without a partner, so I seized my chance and tapped her on the shoulder.

All these sounds and splendours, the comic and pathetic ado of life, had quite bewildered me, and my head was spinning. True, a great deal had happened in the last hour: a disclosure, certainly, although it was not quite clear of what. I hadn't really learnt anything new. Maria Venera loved Trubia to the point of scandal. Evidently. She had gone so far as to have a baby by him. Or what would have been a baby. Yes, she *had* run away with Galfo, but only out of savage obstinacy, an urge to play the fool to vent her negritude of heart. And me? I had come along in time to close the square, a rearguard, a plodding baggage-train, a postman to be exploited and forgotten, a teacher to be cajoled and paid off with a kiss or two. And above all an outsider, worthy of scant regard. For, although I had now taken root in this town through the soles of my two feet, I had not ceased to feel around me an aura of subtle, incorporeal extraneousness, which impregnated my clothes, vocabulary, accent and attitudes, and made me incommensurable with anyone at all who was a relative or fellow-townsman of Venera's. I had come from somewhere else, and not even love could have bleached out this guiltless stain. Furthermore, Venera didn't love me.

She turned.

"Well, professore. Did you see that? Did you hear all?"

She put her arm in mine, steering me across to where the garden fell away into the black valley. She turned her back on the light. After a while I realized she was crying, leaning out over the railing from the waist, like someone being seasick over the side.

"What a difficult girl you are," I said, standing behind her.

"Nonsense. I'm easy," she replied without looking round. "You've got me all wrong."

I pretended to misunderstand her.

"Easy? That'll be the day!"

She bristled, and I went on: "Marry me," I urged her again, laying a hand on her shoulder just where the shoulder-strap faintly grooved her warm-tinted flesh.

She shook her head twice, then asked for a cigarette.

But they were already calling her to join them. The "odd man out dance" was beginning, and they couldn't do without her. Another game, an excuse for making fun of someone. Seven men and six girls were chosen, and the odd man out was given a candle as a mock sceptre. It was his business to palm this off on another fellow, thereby pinching his partner. When the music suddenly cut out, one of the seven was left standing partnerless, spent candle in hand. Need I tell you who ended up the laughing-stock? Although personally I was persuaded that I'd gone out of my way to put myself at a disadvantage for the finish, had hesitated almost on purpose before handing on the baton . . .

An emblem there? A small-change version of my defeat? Now August ends, soon comes September, October . . . Off to a new school, maybe, a new town; a year older and empty-handed. To my aid came the compassion of Maria Venera, affectionate at last. She wanted to dance the slow foxtrot with me, a dance in which I would provoke the fewest disasters. Galfo was on the floor with someone who danced as well as he did, and they were putting on a show. As they passed close by us I thought for a moment he was going to send me his seconds again . . . But instead, he said hullo to Venera, and she said hullo to him. We ended up together at the buffet, signing a peace treaty in the form of three drinks, which became five when we were joined by Iaccarino, still exuding his philosophic vapours.

"If He existed, the word would have got around," he kept muttering, more to himself than to us, in an effort to convince himself; then he melted away into the crowd.

I am pretty sure it was the first time Venera and Galfo had met since the elopement. It was a revolution also, in the traditions of our province, that they should ever again exchange a word in public. And yet, who knows why, everyone seemed to find it perfectly right and proper. A sure sign that the War had begun to change us, we of the island, when an elopement, even if scaled down to a night's outing with no bloodshed, could be pigeon-holed as an escapade to be dismissed from mind. Although in Venera's case the circumstances were exceptional. She had achieved a place on a capacious pedestal which she thoroughly deserved, and ordinary prejudices didn't apply to her. She was the radiant blazon of the city, an epic heroine, an Angelica who seemed each time she descended to this earth to bear the bridle of a Hippogriff in hand.

In the same way, her previous amours (I later learnt that these had been several, more than I suspected or feared) had in the eyes of everybody taken their place within a sort of plausible scheme of things, a fitting and already composed scenario from which there was no escape. For in the destiny of her beauty were contained all the articles of absolution, both civil and penal, and our task was merely to apply them.

This, in ingenuous terms, was what Liborio Galfo attempted to explain to me as soon as Venera had swept off with someone else, and we were left alone together. And then it was, after listening for ten minutes, that I came to understand of what sweet stuff that man was made. Servitude was a thing he needed as a blind man needs his stick; and he was, rather than in love with Venera, her vassal and fanatic, ever since the fateful moment when they stood on a podium together to receive a fake-gold cup after a dancing competition . . . So that now he followed her among the crowd with idolizing eyes, reconciled to me by our mutual struggle and subjection.

"How well she dances," he murmured with devotion into my ear, seeing her bring off a double chassé and immediately flash a dazzling smile at her partner. No use feeling sorry for Galfo. Was his blind devotion worth any less than mine?

Impossible at that moment to imagine that I would meet him thirty years later, run to fat, a placid grandfather holding the hands of a brace of snotty-nosed brats, beneath the bust of Carlo Papa. He simply couldn't place me, so that after the barest courtesies it was a relief to say goodbye (and to think how my heart melts at a homecoming, the haunts of yesteryear . . .). A mite slimmer he was, in his linen get-up, that night in August, as he poured forth his generous floods of passion.

Iaccarino had taken note of this pouring forth, and had been buzzing around him for some time in the hope of being offered another drink. I happened upon them later at the exit, in a weepy embrace; then, propping each other up, they left the party early.

FIFTEEN

End of the Ball and funebrial quadrille.

Isolina, oh how I would have liked a word or two with her! I caught an occasional glimpse of part of her in a welter of bodies and faces, a wisp of skirt, a trusting smile, the flash of a question on a little face swiftly hidden from me by the back of Licausi's neck. Eighty per cent in Italian – pretty hot stuff. I already knew she read a lot. In the school library I had often come across her signature above mine in the register of loans, and cast an eye over her selections, which vacillated between the loftiest poetry and light escapist fiction. Now her leanings were clearly towards the latter, in the person of Saro Licausi. A pleasant enough fellow, since he had let his heart take fire like a normal mortal; but hardly sufficiently so to spark off in anyone that mixture of terror, self-abandon, and astonishment that is the common indication of love. So I was disgusted by the way the girl succumbed to his attentions. It caused me a kind of malaise, a smarting of the heart, from which I drew the conclusion that I was jealous. Jealous without rhyme or reason of course. I wasn't even in love. To put it baldly I was green with envy. For my youth, that evening, I was grasping like a sword, and felt it to be mine, right here, in the gyrations of my blood, within the confines of my body, in the intermittent flashes of my thought. But I had no idea what to do with it, to whom to offer it . . . It was a drug on the market, loot too hot for any receiver. I knew that that evening was the sovereign opportunity of the year, of the summer, of my life, with which tomorrow, or as an old man, to remind myself that I had once been young and alive. I knew that tomorrow I would say it and believe it anyway, but that I would be lying. It wasn't true, I wasn't alive; but he, Licausi, was.

I was in the middle of the dance-floor, still clutching my mock sceptre, my stub of snuffed-out candle; alone, I, and all the rest paired off. I plucked up courage. Licausi was dumbstruck when I asked Isolina for a dance, but relaxed when he saw me give one of my famous gambler's winks, by which I meant to tell him, though only half sincerely, that my invitation was on the level, that I wasn't out to double-cross him, but only to get the low-down on what kind of girl she was, in view of the next, inevitable, friendly, mutual advisory bureau around Mariccia's table. Whereupon Isolina and I began to dance *Quizás, quizás, quizás*.

She was tense, I couldn't imagine why.

"Splendid results," I teased her, "but what do you expect from such a susceptible board of examiners?"

She gazed up at me, little half-pint that she was, and the movement sketched the soft curve of her neck flexing to the high relief of her chin. Next moment she lowered her face, listening without looking at me. And the see-saw of her head was like the rhythmical rocking of a little boat riding close to a lake shore.

I felt that I held prisoner in my arms a gauzy butterfly, more a garment than a girl, even if I only had to press my hand hard against her side to feel, beneath the shield of fabric, a warmth of pliant, neighbouring, unattainable flesh.

We danced awhile in silence. I let my eyes rest on the tint of her cheeks, the ebony of her hair, her large, ingenuous blue eyes. And I set myself to open every sluice-gate within me, before they all gave way before the rush of my heart's floodwaters . . . She was diffident, stand-offish, on the defensive, every so often hitching up her right shoulder-strap, which had a tendency to slip. At last she spoke.

"So I'm a lake, am I?" she asked without looking at me. And, fresh from her studies, "Am I little like Lake Iseo, or large like Garda?" Quickly adding, "And Venera, what lake is she?"

"Venera? Oh, Venera, she's a sea." I tossed the words off with assumed nonchalance, but continued to milk that gentle metaphor to see if I could wring another drop from it. I drew a blank and in desperation I said in the end, "In your waters, though, there's no lack of fishermen."

This with a glance at Licausi, who from the edge of the dance-floor was tracking us with tiger's eyes. Isolina gave a half smile, half pout. I asked what she was going on to study, and where. Literature, at Catania. I thought so. Pity she hadn't been in my course. She nodded. Yes, she'd have liked that too. They said I was good at explaining poetry. Leopardi? Her favourite. She even found him physically attractive, judging from the portrait in the Pedrina anthology. More attractive than Foscolo, that brigand, that Casanova.

Her voice had a veiled, sensual inflection, a guilty ring to it, which contradicted the chaste expression in her eyes, the innocent signet of her limbs in the casket of her balloon skirt. I must admit, if I'd had no scruples about doing the dirty on Licausi . . .

"I have a confession to make," she said, out of the blue. Then, suddenly scared, she changed her mind: "No, no!" And when I pressed her, "Nothing, nothing at all. Just a silly nonsense," she said, then turned the conversation to the song being crooned by a phoney Spaniard. I lent an ear. The music was gently insistent, overriding the shuffle of feet on the paved floor. My lips were grazing her hair, I was stirred by a tenderness towards her, the sapling of her body swaying in my hands.

Siempre que te pregunto
qué, cuándo, cómo y dónde,
tú siempre me respondes
quizás, quizás, quizás . . .

Quizás? Who knows if I don't love this Isolina a little bit? Who knows if she doesn't love me a little? Who knows what love is? Here we are, the two of us, asking ourselves the question and getting no answer, the pseudo-young man and the stripling girl, both of us careering towards the selfsame X, but as sundered as two parallel lines. Who knows if they can love each other, two parallel lines? Myself being in love as my profession, but specializing in inexpedient loves, every word, gesture, or feeling transmuted in me into a parody of a word, a gesture, or a feeling; herself, the other, enclosed in her unfathomable eighteen years, her eyes speaking me yes to no purpose . . . If only I had the gift – and it *is* a gift – of playing the Gay Lothario. How I would love to coax her into mutual lasciviousness! How dexterously would I peel off her clothes, what syllables would I invent to inflame her mind!

O downy arsenals of beauty, frail shields of chiffon ripped by bold fingertip, ruby-red slippers, amber wrap-arounds, hands, and cheeks, and indulgent arms, casques of black tresses on brows of blood-warm marble . . . O professore, how can you not be incited by it? Or do you know a better remedy for the stone which grinds us down? A millstone is this life, sluggish at times, racing at others. And at random it grinds down destiny and chance, the troubles and truces of the blood and of nature, farragos of death and of abundance – trees, torrents, meteors . . . and men. Guilty, all of us; all, from the first to the last, waiting for the chop. Until no one is left, neither little Indians nor big ones. Not even you, professore, who *will* go pawing the ground so! As if you didn't know that suicides are merely short on patience.

Estás perdiendo el tiempo
pensando, pensando,
por lo que tú más quieras
hasta cuando, hasta cuando . . .

Hasta cuando, Isolina? *Quousque tandem*, Cecilia, Venera? Women, women, O ye eternal gods, how long?

Venera, I learnt too late about your name-day celebrations, July 25th, at Acireale, in honour of the saint who bears your name. If I'd known earlier I'd have gone to beg mercy. I'm told that they go in procession bearing a litter of pure silver, engraved and embossed, with your statue riding upon it, answering the prayers of the faithful . . . O Santa Venera, have mercy on me!

Maria Venera, worse luck, knew no more of my thoughts than was guessed at by Isolina. She was hugger-mugger in conversation with Michel, and I had the scant consolation of observing that her dress, where it bordered on the white skin under the arm-pit, was bathed with moisture. Yes, Santa Venera was sweating. Maybe musk and patchouli were not her only perfumes . . .

She was aware from where she stood that I was partnering Isolina, and nodded her approval as if bestowing charity on me, the snub of a temporary leave of absence. More than ever was I convinced that she cared nothing for me, and I tried to avoid that futile dialogue of glances. I barged about among the couples, clumsy as ever, but without any major collisions; some invisible angel was guiding my steps. But I didn't open my mouth, engrossed as I was in further belly-aching about existence, about myself, about how and whence I had sneaked in among men, an alien upon earth, of alien tongue. A far cry, this, from the pirate boarding the royal galleon of life! No, just a miserable Uskok, a buccaneer without a berth, reduced to haphazard coasting from one treasureless island to another. Isolina, now *she* is an island; her very name proclaims it: little island, a little treasure islet. But, if I wished to set foot there, I would have not only to usurp the flag now flying, but also to slough off the whole credo of my pain, to remake myself, spontaneous, stripped bare, a boy again. That's a hard wash for a heart of such old cloth as mine. Perhaps if I had the courage, and a slice of wishful thinking to help me, I might even manage it. Only that August now is at its height; there was a rumble of thunder above us a while ago – they heard it every one. It is the gong – don't kid yourself – for the end of the holidays. And not only that, not only that . . .

I restored Isolina to Licausi. The fingers she held out to me on parting had no relish in them; nor would a pin have passed between her lips. I didn't know what to think of the look she gave me, as she set off again to circle the floor with him. Desolation and relief were written in it; it contained an imperious demand for help, a mild reproof, an insult.

So I found myself alone again, my back to the shrubbery. I thought away and smoked away and watched the others dancing. Until Don Alvise elbowed me in the ribs. He was in a predicament: he couldn't find the lavatory.

"*Comment pissez-vous?*" he asked on his return. "*Moi, je pisse très mal.*"

At four o'clock precisely the quadrille began. It was a concession, both tender and ironic, on the part of the young towards their elders, a stratagem to soothe the stormy seas of the years. The young knew that the sambas and mambas of their day would soon become the dances of the old folks. And so? So, smiling and dutiful, the couples took their places. The quadrille is a figured dance, a type of square-dance requiring a caller. The commands are given in French, the troop obeys, the bandsmen blow their hearts out into their instruments.

It was soon clear that chartered-accountant Ficicchia was not up to the job. His French was hypothetical – *Aux places* came out as *Oblàs*, *Tournoyez* as *Turdumè*. Moreover, his joky attempts at translation aroused no enthusiasm: "Without a mite of fuss or bother/Leave one gent and take another." Or else, "If your partner throws a fit/Get her to walk it off a bit."

No, not a smile, either from the parents or the children, and the "fuss and bother" he hoped to avert took place. So great a chaos that (once a teacher always a teacher) I was reminded of Niccolò Machiavelli at Giovanni dei Medici's manoeuvres.

Licausi, having finally returned his girl to her family table, joined me and anxiously probed me: what was my impression of her? Was she marriageable?

I eluded him with a "Tell you tomorrow at Mariccia's."

In the general confusion I escaped with the excuse that I had to look after Don Alvise. But nothing could stop the old boy now. At the very first note of his beloved Lancers he was on his feet, shaking off the torpor which for the last hour had restored him to his infancy in the cradle of his chair. He was standing bolt upright, drinking in the air through flared nostrils, champing at the bit. I couldn't hold him when, on the lips of the accountant, an order more imbecile than the rest inextricably embroiled the dancers out on the floor. There and then Alvise threw himself on the culprit, thrust him aside and, since he had his stick with him, claimed the right to use it as a baton for the rest of the evening; and with barely a couple of directions reduced the erring spirits to obedience. He had clambered onto a low dais, from which, as from a throne, he thundered, "*Tournoyez*," "*Balancez*," "*Changez les dames*" . . .

The squires and their dames thereupon scurried back into line, hasty, happy pawns in the game, intoxicated by the patterns they created, as if they were getting a bird's eye view of them, and relishing their piquant grace. Each figure perished and was reborn, dovetailed into the next, or issued forth from it, reined in and running free, similar in its renewals to the infinite renewals of the sea.

"*Chacun à sa place*" . . . Don Alvise's voice rose above the noise of the band and the cohorts of feet on the floor.

"*Dansez*" . . . the couples danced.

"*Tournoyez*" . . . the couples parted, circling round each other and around the floor.

"*Balancez*" . . . they rocked and swayed.

"*Grand scène*" . . . they linked arms, they parted, each dancer's hand glancing against his partner's side.

"*En avant, en arrière*" . . . facing each other in two rows the men and women mimicked the eternal to-and-fro of love.

"*Changez les dames*" . . . At this command each squire relinquished his lady and with flowing elegance enveloped her neighbour. But Don Alvise seized that moment to kidnap the first to come his way, wresting her from her rightful partner and plunging into the fray in person. He survived but an instant or two, then hastily gave the order for "*Promenade*", to allow himself a little respite; and he halted, panting, in the middle of the floor. Maria Venera, sweeping by, gave him a smile of encouragement. On her head she wore a diadem of flowers recently bestowed on her. Although another girl, a Plain Jane, had been chosen queen of the ball for a lark, Venera had received the floral tribute, which was the most prized; and on her dark mane, with modesty, she bore its sweetly-scented profusion.

But Don Alvise would not give in. Once more he raised his arms heavenwards, for all the world like the two flapping sleeves of a scarecrow. He signalled to the band, who showed signs of wanting to pack it in, and the dance began again. Step after step they measured, figure after figure, weaving a mobile labyrinth on the floor, with merriment all round, and one big smile of hearty, overheated faces; yes, a good-naturedness, a general feeling of forgiveness, a friendly benevolence . . .

"*Balancez . . . Balancez . . . Balancez.*" Like a record stuck in the groove Don Alvise's voice seemed spellbound. His waxen face first turned the colour of earth, then flushed a dirty purple. The dancers, oblivious, even when the band cut out, continued mechanically to go through their paces, as they saw the old man row with his arms, clutch at the empty air before him as if to grapple a non-existent partner; and then with the crash of a lofty tree pitch down.

SIXTEEN

Taking leave of Don Alvise.
Visit to Via Carreri.
Unwilling visit to Don Nitto.

Removing Don Alvise was no easy matter. We had to resort to the largest available car in order to accommodate the sprawling, distorted body. Three of us went with him: myself, ever at home with death, plus the two grand-children at daggers drawn, who in the emergency of this unforeseen event appeared to have buried the hatchet and stoked up the family patriotism. Sasà, tight-lipped at the wheel, bridled his feelings with an effort. Venera, on the other hand, sobbed inconsolably, clasping the old man's hands in hers, interrogating his closed eyes and the negligible wisp of breath between his sagging lips. He seemed pretty much a goner, Alvise, so we trod on it all the harder, hoping to reach the nearest first-aid post. Looking at the girl, I thought how much she must be dreading her imminent solitude in the empty palazzo; but I suspected even more that her tears were an outlet for all the rage that had smouldered in her these recent weeks, and for the passions of the night. A night now fading before our eyes, mottled with rosy spots that shifted, as if wind-wafted, out of the orient towards the perlaceous sky of the seashore.

We overtook a jeep, the unsleeping jeep of the location-hunting Parisians. Through the side-window, in the trice before the dust engulfed them, Michel's blue eyes grew wide with astonishment as they lit on Venera and Alvise in the pose of a Pietà . . .

By the time we reached the hospital gates, human hands could do no more for him: Don Alvise was dead. Our remaining task was to take him home to the palazzo in Upper Módica, to help him climb the old stairs for the last time, Sasà and me, holding the head and feet of him, lugging him up like a piece of furniture. Then the neighbours flocked in, the two Trubia daughters came running, the other grand-children took him over; and at last he vanished into his own rooms for the laying out and the ritual wake.

Day was upon us in the meantime, and the electric light, vanquished by nature's own, looked tawdry and unreal, so I switched it off. We were left in the pallor of dawn, the three of us, me on my feet and the two cousins seated, watching the murky strip of morning scheming unfathomable prognoses on the wall. My thoughts ran on death, on my heart beating mulishly away, though every fibre in me cried out to die; and on Don Alvise, and the treasury of memories lost beneath the tombstone of his brow.

Venera and Sasà Trubia sat face to face in silence, looking as though they were waiting for me to leave. Not so. For when I made a move to go, Venera summoned me back, wanted me at her side. Then, from a drawer I recognized, she took out the bundle of dried blood and handed it to Trubia.

"This, dear cousin," she said, "belongs to you."

The funeral was of the best: the whole of Módica was there. Alvise, may the earth lie light upon you!

According to Venera's wishes, the old boy's booty of stockings and shoes, treasured by him under the glass bell, was laid in the coffin with him, and she placed the walnut stick in his hands, for him to hook at the ankles of the shades in Hades. Puck, who had been really attached to him, walked at my side along with Anita the maid, behind the cortège of blood-relations. In which his grand-daughter stood out, crowning her mourning weeds with a chalk-white face, most beautiful. Tall between her two aunts, and on the arm of Sasà, with an air of ferocious and sorrowful triumph, in her cousin's company she might have been approaching the altar. No one in the crowd dared utter a word of comment. The clash of two evenings ago, slaps and spittle included, would doubtless tomorrow be the occasion of hilarious myth-making within the four walls of the Conservative Club, but in the meanwhile Venera was acting a death-scene, and deserved an ovation.

It was at that instant, as I looked at her, while stepping in time with the mournful cadences of the band, that I realized I had already spoken all my lines, that I was once more sitting with the rest of them, a spectator in the familiar "gods". My love for Venera had deflated like a sail, and I felt unfettered, set free from her and from all and sundry, supposing I had ever really loved any of them. So far, I was beginning to persuade myself, I had not really loved, but only *wanted* to love. And choosing only trumped-up images into the bargain: a Venera out of the Song of Songs, whose weirdness of sentiment might equally have masked a trivial mystery or a grandiose one; a Cecilia Persephone, whose rare and melancholy speech alone had enabled her to remain deiform in my thoughts; but from whom I now received daily postcards dispatched from places which were not the Elysian Fields but, at most, Peschiera, Verona, Custoza . . . She must be in cahoots with a Lombard-Venetian travelling salesman, or else a historian of the Italian Risorgimento . . . And then this Isolina, bride-to-be and destined mother-of-many, whom I already imagined unbuttoning her blouse to offer, to a swarm of bawling twins, her girlish breast. Theatricals, no more than that. All I had done was play-act love, mime out inevitable love in the scenario of inevitable life. Exposed on my own to the derision of the footlights, my lines squelchy with tears, my nerves all of a jitter, and with the joys and the smarts of the heart. A stand-in playing the lead among a mass of fawning extras. Starting with Iaccarino and Madama (ah, the recreants!), black bags under their eyes and love-bites red on their necks. Then Colombina, Rosaura, Zanetta and all, so enamouring, so enamoured, all strolling players along with me in the first, fateful, exonerating and ultimate tournée of my youth . . .

Think, just a year or two after the war. But how long ago that seemed, what a century ago, that filthy war, that filthy death! We were reborn convalescent in the sun. And more than that: deathless, invulnerable in the one heel and the other. And you also, my Sicily, belovèd isle, you painted your lips and flirted again with life under a sun that noticed nothing, that knows nothing of invasions, devastations, mafias, but indiscriminately breeds both the wasps on this basket of figs and the flies on the face of that slain man sprawled beneath a lop-sided olive. In Palermo they are muttering prayers again, in the churches and within the courts of the mighty: "Our Father which art in heaven," "Our godfather which art on earth" . . . These today, tomorrow, and for ever, are the paternosters of the Conca d'Oro . . . But in that case, what was I to do? I, Gingolph the Forsaken, Guerin the Downcast? The inept, the hectic, pleonastic, at-death's-doorly I? A hawker, a pedlar, a puppet of love. Indeed, the puppet-show posters should read:

"In the first scene we observe Gesualdo, alias the Downcast, who meets the Ogre and kisses his hands. The Love-Ogre gobbles him up. He gobbles him up but spits him out again, as the whale spat out Jonah."

What! Hell! what are you clapping for? Go to the devil!

Right, let's step down a rung. Two, in fact. Truth is that after the funeral I went, all alone alone-O, into the shadows of Via Carreri, site of the most frequented whorehouse in Módica, with its top-class girls all scrubbed and scented and professional. I'd been there a couple of times with Iaccarino – a regular customer, practically a season-ticket holder – but I'd always stayed in the lobby and politely fought off the ritual solicitings:

"Fancy me? I'm Dolores."

"How d'you like it? *Alla bolognese*?"

"Come on boy, the whole hog!"

By heart I knew the ending of *L'Éducation sentimentale*, and often used to quote it to my friends, so as to refute it: "Those days, perhaps, were the best days of our lives." No, for me it was not like that, and to induce me to cross that threshold, even reluctantly, it took an irresistible surging within me.

Nevertheless, this time I went there full of purpose, as a man might go to buy himself a revolver. And within me a low-keyed, quiet longing, without the least qualm of conscience.

The room was a-reek with perfumes, and dim, almost in darkness, had it not been for the lemon-tree in a pot, with its impetuous country lustre. The girl was skinny, still pretty beneath her mask of make-up. From Portici, she said.

"I can see you're a gentleman. The slobs pick the fat ones," she flattered me, in an accent a pastiche of Naples and every other place in her twenty-year wanderings from top to toe of the peninsula. I remember the *rip* of a zipper, and that vision of a garment falling, flicked off by a deft, simple movement of the knee, swiftly . . . Afterwards I couldn't help being sick into the wash-basin. Not from disgust – it had been nice – but from the purely mechanical mutiny of an overworked system. I lingered, all the same, to run my eye over the feminine knick-knacks on the chest-of-drawers. The little bits and pieces carefully arranged to give herself a feeling of permanence and possession, as if the law didn't move these girls on every two weeks in any case. Like us, I thought, like us in this world for our scurrying fortnight . . .

On our way down, just for something to say, "We've been in Seventh Heaven," I remarked, pointing up at the many flights of stairs.

"In hell, you mean," she replied, without any tragic overtones; and, handing her tag to Zoë behind the counter, she reclimbed the stairs.

Back in town, a shower caught me: sporadic drops, large and warm, children of a passing storm. I had to take refuge in the Caffè Buonaiuto, where on a marble table-top a newspaper promised peace in Korea and the return of Einaudi and De Gasperi from their holiday havens: the President from Ponte San Martino,the Prime Minister from Val Sugana. They must have had it cool up there, awoken early by the diplomatic courier or whatever. All unawares that . . .

O time, how it rots not only bodies but events, the whys and wherefores of every human act. Give it a year or two and everything that happens is debunked, is robbed of meaning, is crusted wih a leprous, ominous saltpetre, scaling off like the skin of a wall. No hope that what is going on this instant will tomorrow have more bite to it than what happened yesterday, be it the Late Massacre in Piedmont, or the Battle of the Somme, or the 18th Parallel . . . Yesterday, blood, toil, tears and sweat; today, subtitles in a textbook.

Santo, the waiter, gave his approval. It was not the first time that, over my coffee, I had involved him in my yelpings, and he generally approved. He took them for profound cogitations, giving me, as to the dog, an extra lump of sugar and loving service in return for the learning I bestowed on him. This time, however, along with the sugar came a message. Don Nitto wished urgently to see me up at La Sorda. Antonio had been calling at the caffè every half-hour, trying to find me.

So I went up to the mansion, albeit with scant enthusiasm. It was time to shut up shop: that rain had been a warning. School would soon be upon us again, with rustlings of pages and motes of dust floating up and down in a single slanting sunbeam. And all those black overalls, and eyes blue, brown, and black beneath girlishly knitted brows . . . Once again I would read out the time-honoured lines, the ancient, delectable syllables, starting from the Provençal poets and their progeny:

Ai, las! tan cuidava saber
d'amor e tant petit en sai!

"You thought you knew so much of love
Alas, how little do you know!"

Everything the same, but a year older, and 'Fifty-One would never return again.

Neither would Módica. I was threatened with a transfer. If this happened, invitations and party-goings were of no further use to me, my brief worldly glory called for no tomorrow, and the Ball at Chiaramonte had been the last of a lifetime. From that moment on I was always to prefer a tranquil sadness to a troubled joy.

There in his customary gazebo, almost his Throne Room, Don Nitto, without getting to his feet, offered me five sticks of flint – his hand. Standing at his side, ex-M.P. Scillieri deemed it sufficient to dangle a couple of fingers at me, with the air of a man offering me a nibble of the Host or a beakerful of manna. They were not alone. At the two extremities of a bench sat our good "Don's" two henchmen, whom I knew by sight. They had come with him from the Vicaría, the Mafia midden of Palermo, and stayed on to infest the mansion in company with Antonio the chauffeur. One of them had a minuscule head poised on a stalk-like neck that appeared to tremble with every breath he took – but as a steel wire trembles; the other had a swart, glabrous face, with short sideburns recently razor-trimmed. They were both spreading jam on vast hunks of bread with broad-bladed knives of the kind the Mafia call "soap-lickers". On a table at centre-stage, a ream of white paper, an inkstand, and a pen – a gold fountain-pen – gave the impression of waiting for someone. I knew at once that the someone was myself.

Nitto made a didactic speech, enunciating each word with care, as if speaking to a class of morons. The ex-Hon. Member was in a position of some delicacy, he said. He had to address an important meeting in two week's time, there were serious matters in the air, signs of an agreement between the Monarchists and the defunct Man-in-the-Street Party. I could not back down.

(Back down? What from? What do these people want from me?)

I stole a glance at the ex-Hon. Member himself. His expression was both crafty and cretinous, with tiny, close-set eyes. I had never addressed a word to him; all I had done was spy on his amorous trafficking, in the company of Madama, from my peephole between two pots of parsley. Though for some time, admittedly, he had been for no apparent reason honouring me with hat-doffings and servilities . . .

What did he want from me? I looked him the question, and with a glance he indicated the paper on the table. Finally he deigned to open his lips.

"Two or three ideas, but meaty. About the country, jobs, freedom. Stress the freedom."

I turned to Don Nitto, protesting that I couldn't do it, that it wasn't in my line. Genuinely distressed he seemed.

"If you really can't . . . If it's not in your line . . ." But sweetly, sadly, he added, "I wouldn't have believed it! You too, as bad as the rest of them – a sponging trickster."

I was baffled.

"Have you forgotten Cecilia?" said he, fondling his plaster neckpiece. "A good girl, that one. Reliable. She does what Daddy tells her. If you like, I'll send her a wire and she'll buzz back."

And, so saying, he put a flea in my ear that I have never since been able to dislodge . . .

Meanwhile the two thugs had got up from the bench and were strolling beneath the trees, occasionally eyeing me with good-humoured curiosity, as butchers might study a fresh side of beef on the marble slab.

There seemed to be no way out. I sat down and started writing.

I slipped in a few whoppers, Scillieri jeopardized his career, and I'm still lying low.

SEVENTEEN

Last days in Módica. Farewell banquet and talk of love. Wedding feast with questionable revelation. Iaccarino at the Belvedere and rainy finale.

Liborio Galfo it was who told me that Maria Venera had left Módica. She had observed the statutory three days cloistered in the house, accepted the funeral baked meats, the visits of the mourners and the rest of it. Then off she'd gone with not a word to anyone but him, and then only a scribbled couple of lines. I was cut to the quick. It was not only a question of love, but of trust: once again she'd made me play second fiddle. After all, she could have mentioned it when, like all the world, I went to express my condolences, and Anita ushered me into the banquet hall, redolent of quinces, where I'd never been before. From the lofty ceiling cupids and sirens blistered with damp occasionally let fall a flake of time-worn paint onto the pitted brick-paved floor. Much dancing had gone on here a century back; there was even a musicians' gallery which, for the players of the time, had served as village Bayreuth, but relegated now to loft-cum-storeroom. Seated on rickety chairs were three or four nondescript consolatrices; and she in the midst of them, stricken with grief, mourner exemplary.

Among those who came in to change the guard with me I was struck by the presence of Michel, the film-johnnie. I'd already noticed him, during the funeral, busy taking photographs from a terrace overlooking the "Salon", but I couldn't imagine what right he had to be here, a foreigner, a stranger. I understood all, later, when Galfo told me that it was with him that Venera had gone off. Not on some madcap impulse, a second elopement (perish the thought!), but prudently, with a solid contract signed and sealed, guaranteeing her a small part in the forthcoming film. Galfo spoke with conviction, and seemed pleased about it.

"This is obviously what she was cut out for," he said. "Better for me too – I wasn't the right husband for her. Just as well you all turned up that night!"

What could I say? I had my own opinion, but kept quiet, even though months later I conscientiously went to the cinema and hunted for Maria Venera's name among the extras in the cast of *Carrosse d'or*. Without finding it, of course. I knew I wouldn't.

So I didn't contradict Galfo. What's more, as he had taken a liking to me, if only in order to talk to me about the girl, whom he was still openly distressed about, I asked him to lunch with me one Sunday. Licausi had for some time been having his meals with his future parents-in-law, and we missed him, Iacca and I, reduced as we were to making up our threesome with the fish. All the more so because I now liked to linger at table through the siesta hour, and even take a seat early, before Mariccia had the food ready. It's common enough this, to recoup with gluttony and idleness at times when there's nothing else going; and now that the heart in my breast had downed tools, I enjoyed just sitting around, being waited on hand and foot, no longer all of a dither and scattering tears to the winds; and leaving to the philosopher – who made full use of it – the monopoly of the conversation. All our contentment lacked was a third to make a trio, and Galfo filled the gap, with his gentle nature, his perpetual sense of wonder.

That Sunday, moreover, my invitation was to a valedictory banquet. For leave I must; the news had appeared in black and white in the Official Gazette, and the headmaster lost no time in passing on the information. I don't know whether he was more pleased or sorry to be rid of such a Johnnie head-in-air . . .

So then, to Módica a long farewell! and to the corner of an Ionian isle in which she lies; to her elegance, her country ways.

To the portals of her churches with their surging tides of steps. To the gentle warmth of her courtyards, her benevolent carob trees. To her stone walls shining as words of God. To the easygoing speech of her people. To her festivals and to her funerals. To the wheat of her fields and the honey of her bees . . .

Lastly, farewell to friends, seated, as the custom is, about a round table . . .

Mariccia worked her fingers to the bone for the occasion, but without much luck. The inky cuttlefish risotto could have done with another minute of attention. To say nothing of the insipid coffee. That was enough to set off Iaccarino who, in common with every Socrates, would turn up his nose at a rotten coffee in favour of a decent tot of hemlock; and who, in addition, had even dreamt he was in for a poor meal. He always dreamt the day's events in advance.

Galfo seconded this: the same thing happened to him. He could have hit on no surer way of maddening my friend, who couldn't stand sharing any privilege whatever, and went so far as to tax the other's premonitions with being a lot of humbug, mere doodles and apparitions wrought in a drowsy mind, the refuse of consciousness.

"I'm different," he maintained. "I'm a sort of warlock. It's in my blood. My grandfather used to climb Etna to gather mandrake root."

And so on and so forth, the usual old extravaganzas.

At last we got to our feet and set off towards the "Salon". But as we neared the War Memorial the conversation turned to Venera, to the character of Venera, and Iacca bestowed on her a few immoderacies of language to which the bronze-faced Unknown Soldier listened without turning a hair. And for peace's sake so did I.

Not so Galfo, gentle fellow though he was.

"Venera," explained Iaccarino, in answer to his protests, "is paroxysmal, like so many Sicilians. We have to forge assets for ourselves and revere them in place of God. Assets and counter-assets. When one of these lets us down we rush to its opposite, idolize it, cash in on it. We never choose the middle way: we go to one extreme or the other, be it devotion or acrimony, trust or suspicion, sealed lips or a wagging tongue, scandal or respectability, honour or dishonour. Yes, I said dishonour. And Venera made that choice out of pride and arrogance, and put her heart into it. She wanted to get her own back for her poverty and her inability to love. Because there's one thing I'm sure of: she never loved even Trubia . . ."

Galfo did not have the gift of the gab. He'd had trouble getting his diploma, and lived off his properties. Nevertheless he felt that Iaccarino's arguments were not entirely sound, and was spitting like a wildcat.

To calm him down I butted in, turning the conversation onto the whole emotion of love. I had formed an idea about it in the last few months, and liked to discuss it, although I was convinced that everyone who forms such an idea is swayed by his own personal vicissitudes, so that what he takes to be a universal law is really only a particular rule which has guided his own steps, as different from other people's rules as one nose is from another.

Now, judging by what had happened to me, love seemed what one might call a transversal emotion, obliquely intersecting all the main highways of the heart of man. In spite of all appearances, never the high street but always a crossing that slices through the heart of us like a crooked sabre, hacking an aperture between the senses, nerves, and imagination, ending in the construction of an emptiness, and of a mask. A distorted emotion based on misunderstanding, on mistaken identity; close, therefore, to the tricks and hypocrisies of actors and poets. So that, coming back to Venera, and trying to judge her dispassionately, my opinion was that she was not the madcap Iaccarino made her out to be, but a little mechanism of unexpected moods, oddly geared to a thirst for deceit. A prejudiced opinion, as I said, and applicable also to myself; indeed, especially to myself, to my teeterings between cowardice and a taste for theatre, poltroon and Pantaloon, doomed to face every love affair as a primadonna must face applause and catcalls alike.

This I clumsily expressed to Iaccarino, who pedantically homilized in turn.

"Love," he stated, "is what you say it is, and more besides. Partly a battle to the death, partly an alliance of victims and tyrants. Culminating, as it does, in the invasion of one by the other, the pouring of one into the other; for the couple of seconds that it lasts love truly resembles the Eucharist, and is just as much of an impious piety . . ."

Galfo would have liked to have his say, but Iaccarino shut him up, agreeing with me that we should delve deeper into this, play four-hands at writing a Code of Love, an Ethics of Love. We agreed that love makes for suffering because it lacks a code of universally accepted rules, such as it used to have in the days of Andrea Cappellano.

At this point there was no plausible reason for delaying our daily bout of billiards, beneath the benevolent eye of Santo the waiter, God rest his soul.

It was Iaccarino yet again who held the floor, months later, at Licausi and Isolina's wedding. This took place around Christmas, and I came in from another town with a dark grey double-breasted suit in my sham-leather suitcase, and bearing a be-ribboned package containing a small silver dish. Before the service at San Giorgio I went up to Madama's to say hullo and ask for half an hour's hospitality in order to change. She wasn't there, and nor was Iaccarino, now her only tenant. The door was opened by a tall girl in glasses, black hair in bangs, the pallor of a nun, and in her arms the cat Quo Vadis? who didn't seem to recognize me.

I introduced myself, and she demurely did likewise. She was Madama's daughter, back from boarding school, and occupying the room that had been mine. She was called Luisa. The look she gave me was calm and hungry, her hand remained in mine for that extra second, soft and firm and flattering. "We'll see about this later," I said to myself, and shut myself in the bathroom to change. Then, when my friend arrived – whom I found more glum, unhappy, and garrulous than ever – dressed as witnesses we set off to face the ceremony.

Here in front of me, thirty years later, I have the menu for the wedding-breakfast at her parents' place, printed on Caran d'Ache card, including the lines Iacca penned for the occasion (copied in fact from an eighteenth-century epithalamium of the most sober tenor). While others I find which are lewd, inscribed on a curious papyrus donated to me by the professor following his return from the lavatory, where he had executed a pencilled impromptu. And between one course and the next, while I fixed my eyes on Isolina, he spouted them into my ear:

> O roll of tissue, silky velveteen,
> Handmaid to the *toilette* of Isoline
> When, 'scaping the golden caves of sleep, she sits
> Down to perform her bodily requisites . . .

Isolina: in my mental group photograph of that day she alone is out of focus. As if memory had censored her on purpose, sent her to Coventry, thrown around her a cordon sanitaire. Maybe with such moments in time the memory behaves as the body does when confronted with an onslaught of microbes. As soon as the infection starts, millions and billions of friendly corpuscles leap to the counter-attack, swarm around the crucial point, isolate it, submerge it, thicken the tissues surrounding it, forming an invincible calcareous crust. I must have read somewhere of lungs in which a hotbed of infection, once incapsulated, struggles on, and dies, and is reborn, practically eternal and practically impotent behind its ramparts. And so it is with memories, I think. A defence force isolates the most dangerous, and leaves them disarmed and dormant within us. Inactive, but alive. Immortal, but inert.

Just so, in my thoughts, Isolina is a dress without a face, a voice without a sound, in among the glitter of bottles and the plates clattering on the tables; while Iaccarino, with his blackguard text in hand, softly at first into my left ear, but then more loudly to the world at large, countering my protests with the justification that even in the most glorious of Triumphs *someone* is required to remind the victorious Consul of the mortality of the flesh, proceeded to recite:

> . . . Because I do not hope to sniff again
> At the florid roses of that ambrosial den,
> Be thou my messenger, act thou for me
> In that proud lady's secret sanctuary . . .

Isolina, Isolina . . . And when, none too sober myself, I started clinking glasses with Iaccarino, and he ploughed ahead with those couplets of his without scandalizing anyone, so little did the faecal meaning emerge through the screen of aureate diction, which itself got lost in the general uproar:

> There, of her heavenly members you will see
> Anon, those brave vibrations each way free,
> The alabastrine candours, the black curls,
> In charming disaccord (girls *will* be girls).
> If then, like bees which intromit the flowers
> From which their honey all its taste acquires,
> She proffers to the bowl's voluptuous kiss
> Her satin, roseate protuberances,
> Then sound hosannas! Scatter pearls and rubies
> On the waters quickened by that ethereal pubes . . .

And so on and so forth until the bridegroom, who knew his Iacca backwards, and was harkening from afar, stabbed two poignard fingers fiercely at Iacca's eyes . . .

And when the pharmacist Fratantonio had a fancy to dance Migliavacca's Mazurka with his pharmacist lady-wife, and they came a cropper, in the middle of the room, both the he and the she of it, and Santo Spagnuolo the photographer slaughtered them with his flashbulb, and everyone cried, "Up with the in-laws, up with the newlyweds!" All but me, all but me . . .

And when I asked news of Venera, and they all said "Hmmph" . . . And when Don Nitto, seated at the head of the table and fanning himself with a fan, was summoned by his chauffeur, and left the room, his face suddenly waxen, and didn't come back; and someone at the window said they'd seen him in the doorway between two policemen, shackled like St Peter-in-Chains . . .

And when they got rid of us all, by dribs and drabs, each with a bonbonnière in hand, and the bride and groom were out on the steps saying their goodbyes, and at each goodbye Canon Ciulla cried "A kiss for the bride!" and Licausi shoved me into her arms, and Isolina on tiptoe met my eyes with her wide astonished blue ones, and my lips with her lips, and the fragrance of cake still on them, and kissed me clumsily, breathing in a whisper, 'Angel, my Archangel" – Or so I thought, or so I thought . . .

What was the finale then? The finale came towards nightfall, when Iacca and I went up to the Belvedere. Módica lay cloven beneath us, a-glitter with the lights of its garrets, a formicary of distant antlings. It wasn't raining yet, but the window-pane of the sky had misted over, and a rough night was brewing. For Licausi as well, I should suppose . . .

Hatless and ripe with wine, we looked down into the cleft of the valley, at the toy houses and tiny people, every one of them with his own peace, his own war, with the grumbling of his blood in arteries hardening every instant.

What's going on down there at this very moment? Sasà Trubia has eaten himself sick and is swilling down calomel and emitting feeble moans on the bosom of Signora Trubia, *née* Virgadauro; Mariccia is re-reading *The Baker's Wife*, syllable by syllable, all unawares that a growth is thriving in her belly like an unwanted child or gaudy melon flower; Anita, as every evening, is standing in the doorway and gazing into Venera's deserted room; Miciacio the night-watchman, nicknamed the Nightjar, is moving from house to house sticking a ticket into the crack of each door, to bear witness to his faithful vigilance; Enza Aloini is one-finger-typing her thesis on Forteguerri's *Ricciardetto*; Peppino Papaleo, as he faces the last flight of stairs, is thinking that this pain in his chest where his heart should be, this gnawing woodworm, why, it's nothing at all, nothing but a touch of nerves; Isolina and Licausi . . .

Think of them all down there, all so busy with living in a perishable Here, an ephemeral Now, an unbegotten December of 'Fifty-One, certain that it's worth it, that living has some meaning to it . . . While I, whiny as ever, *yelp yelp*, and drunk into the bargain, almost as drunk as Iacca . . . Whom I would dearly like to pick a bone with for laying claim to that anonymous letter, whereas . . . Isolina, Isolina, did you love me, then? Your Angel, Archangel, was that really me? Or else, once again, is it only a lark? And anyway, does it matter at all? To me, what does it matter?

All this I wanted to say to the philosopher, and I started to say it, as one pissed newt to another, for at such times one is at one's most weighty. He shot me a wrathful, knavish look, and I don't know what he'd have said in his defence, because at that moment, above and below us, the hundred, the thousand bells of Módica pealed forth, rung by a hundred, a thousand bell-ringers – a clappered pandemonium, the incontrovertible herald of the end of the world.

And then, unbelievably, amidst the first few streamers of rain we saw a scatter of birds from the rooftops, and the statues stepped down from their niches, started to walk. And a roll of thunder seemed to pursue them, starting from here above, from the two of us, and spreading and spreading like the whorls of a whirlpool, until it reached the most distant borders of the County of Módica – Frigintini, Mussomeli, Pozzallo, Scornavacche – and the fishing-boats heard it out at sea, and on the Irminio bridge a carter drew rein under a lowering cloud: Alas, O Lord, the tempest is upon us, what will become of me?

When silence returned I saw Iaccarino on his knees. He always ended up on his knees when he'd drunk too much. He would never have been that humble, he used to say, without a bit of Dutch courage. But now the rain was belting down, and he on his knees, a hunched-up, terror-striken mite of a man, huddled into his body as into someone else's overcoat, his back towards me, printing on the flashing backdrop of the sky a silhouette like that of Job, of a plaintive Moses; and he upon his knees haranguing God.

"Come on, let's go," I said, as I stood behind him sheltering him with Madama's umbrella, which I'd had the foresight to bring with me. He didn't answer. He now was talking to God, and I felt I was eavesdropping on a squabble between two litigants in court. I heard him beseeching and cursing, and tootling his puny posthorn to the four corners of the sky.

"Hey you! I saw you there! Don't try and get smart with me! Don't pretend you don't exist! God, exist, I beg of you! I command you to exist!"

He got no answer, unless it was the Morse code drummed on the car roof by the rain.

I had to drag him away by force.

SIXTH ASIDE

Exit.

Dear reader, sweet summer, we must say farewell. Once upon a time there was a boy who thought he was an old fogy, but now the roles are reversed, and the fogy has feigned boyhood, and to deceive himself the better has draped all the mirrors in the house with rags. Permissible expedients these, if not essential. After all, I have written to assuage old age, and proposed this emotional motion to none but myself. But something it must mean, if those bygone days still rain a flaxen gold-dust in my memory. Sometimes I feel I'm growing old manacled to this memory of mine, as guardian dragons wax old beside their treasure-hoards, with never a single paladin coming to challenge them. Poor, wrinkly old dragons, their bodies scaly as the bark of ancient olives, imprisoned in the dark, waiting only for the flash of some Excalibur before their eyes to bring them recompense for all their patience. While the years roll by, and a green mould crusts the copper bosses on the coffers, and a drop from the rock roof of the cavern, at lengthy intervals, metes out for them both time and silence.

Here in the middle of my forehead there is a place a millionth of an inch across, where that summer slept with sixty others, and where it will now go sleeping once again, with all its flauntings of phoney glory, its flunked exultancies of clouds and flowers, its bodies embalmed and bandaged like young pharoahs. Every one of them a Lazarus who won't lie down, both the young and the old, including Alvise, who never tires of coming to tick me off, impervious to the fact that we buried him on page 151.

"You're lord and master here," he insists, pooh-poohing my

objections. "No skin off *your* nose if you bring me back to life."

How can I refuse such a firmly-based petition.

"Let's invent a past," suggested Tiddlypush that August night.

"Let's invent a future!" was my comeback.

Is it possible to deny a person, even in the very act of loving them? One of those saints did it, before the cock crew thrice . . . But I? . . .

"A mechanical substitute for life," said I. And here you have it. It's gone phut, but all the same . . .

For a month or two it worked. It was basically as if, for my own benefit, I was repeating Scheherazade's famous trick – telling stories to stay alive. And for a while it worked. I would sleep five hours at a stretch – nothing less than a miracle. And I dreamt dreams packed full of flights, flights low over roseate foam where with slow and easy strokes I swam. Women, walking on the water, came smiling to greet me. I had friends, in short, and underlings, and accomplices – a motherland. Every character I invented, or transcribed from memory, breathed a warm, moist breath upon my cheek, like the breath of a newborn beastling. Then down he would sit at my bedside, and he consoled me, I consoled him. I even began to talk to myself again, which is my greatest joy.

I made my plans with the meticulous foresight of a strategist, a Don Juan, a tourist, an assassin. Designing, first of all, as a setting for my simulations, a real town in a real place, in which, however, from the main crossroads branched dead ends, blind alleys, irretrievable footsteps. I peopled it then with presences, an ambulating archive, with identity photos of all and sundry, their dossiers past and present, horoscopes, false teeth, colour of neckties and quaint idiosyncrasies of speech.

For the plot, a file to itself. It was coming along nicely, a droll little anecdote, with about as much rhyme as reason, as true and as distorted as life itself. With a thousand pretty little booby-traps to make the party go: decoys for ducks, birdlime for skylarks, hook-line-and-sinkers for codfish in blinkers. What more can I say? A rare old gallimaufry, a medley of vaudeville and grand opera, scat vocals and bel canto, according to my strength of pulse and expense of spirit, though emulating first and foremost the art of the puppeteer. And all set at a juicy time in history, albeit no more stable than a vision is. With interchangeable characters, each one as tricksome as transitory, like the nudes at the *Folies Bergères* seen intermittently in the flashing lights. A text full of falsettos, affectations, consolations, concealed quotations, titters, tatters and student rags . . . But not short on outcries, heartcries, even tears. Something to match the position I am in this minute, my own deceiver and sycophant, my own librarian of nothingness; me, out-of-work custodian in an Alexandria in ashes, lying here tonight, sixty years old, a reasonable age to be dying, not so to be writing, on a double-bed in a doss-house, waiting for dawn and totting up words like a skinflint his shekels, with weary pen on the snow-blank back of a map of the city.

Words, words, words . . . Or perhaps I ought to call them the chronicles of my catastrophe, the dross and dregs of memory, the knocks the postman always takes, words which tomorrow the Grand Inquisitor will hear – one ear blocked with wax and the other bunged with an earplug. Ah yes, words . . . I drew up a whole glossary of them, almost the roster of an army, words depraved and timorous and arrogant and full of sorrow, all of them toeing the line until it sickens you. In one passage – and I'm not telling you where – I fought at their head in a variant of the Battle of Zama. After picking my men in advance, half by choice and half by chance, I drew them up in squares and phalanxes, and blistered their feet with my *Grandes Manoeuvres*. Tinkering with the facts to suit the words, and milking the words for facts. Of such small matter are the facts of the matter. So the upshot, you may be sure, was a ready-made dossier of words, verbs, adverbs, deverbatives, proverbs. Just for a laugh, dear reader, I offer you a derisory selection: amaranthus, cinnabar, malachite, panoply, adumbrate, deliquium, mellowly, fallow, halcyon, jasmine, iridescent, tamarind, albion, puissant, sarabande, welkin, emerald, aspen, indigo, silverling, jubilant, malkin, caramel, periwinkle, alchemy, colonnade, anodyne, relinquish, florin, lambent, sibling, chalcedony, celandine, paladin, purlieus, parentheses . . .

The aim was to discharge onto myself, as my own stand-in and stunt-man, the debts of myself as narrator, paying them off by playing them off. And for a while it worked. One day, when I'd had fun dressing you all up as a clacque of clappers, I fell asleep with my head on the table; something that hadn't happened since I was a boy. Oh yes, writing has been both a guilelessness and a bolt-hole, a throne within a bolt-hole, and I will never thank myself enough for having had the courage to do it.

Until a mob of rummy characters came creeping into it. Rummy like our noses look when we squidge them flat against a mirror. And they used my tongue to talk with, but spoke someone else's words: the words of an enemy, of a dwarf jester, of a strident, acidulous scribe. You will find his slobber all over the place. I haven't even attempted to wipe it off.

After him, the deluge. And, if I must confess all, some of the blame is mine. For I myself, who now say I, *Ego scriptor, Ego scriba, Ego es, Ego ego*, scrambled Ego, bred within me a rabble of traitors, who laid plots against me and, key at the ready, as soon as my back was turned unlocked the stable door . . . To be frank, one fine morning I found (written when? between sleep and waking? and by whom, if not by *him*, or *them*?) the pages of a new chapter half blocked in and foreboding a sticky end for the hero. An end, still worse, both deadly and voluntary. There was even a stirring epitaph "written in a country churchyard . . ."

The only option, plainly, was to commit that page to the flames. And so I did. However, from my youth up I had been tempted by the idea of making a totally blank book, entitled *Omissis* and signed Anon . . . And when anyone teased me about being arty and "going all Mallarmé", I would reply that no, I did not aspire to Nothingness *ne varietur*, the Immaculate Conception as explained to the populace. No, this was my fashion of raising a silent finger to say that life hurt me but I didn't have the guts to take it out on anyone. If indeed it wasn't a cry for help, an unconditional surrender . . . Like an ambulance with sirens blaring and a hand at the window piteously begging room to pass, or a rifle poking up from a trench, and knotted to the muzzle there's the white flutter of a hanky.

Well then, I burnt that page. But not the others, the earlier effigies in my personal Madame Tussaud's. Although for years I had yearned for an ashless cremation, clean as only death can make it; although I believed that death indeed is the final accountant and auditor authorized to redress the intemperances of destiny and the dirty cards she deals you from the bottom of the pack. There is no guarantee like death's guarantee to make peace between me and you, dear reader, between just us two, the Unhappy Few, the only me, the only you . . .

I don't quite know why, but I didn't play that chip. Camping in my manuscript as in a leaky tent, numbed by innumerable nights beneath the stars, beta-blocked by drugs as a car by a handbrake, helpless – save with a pitchfork – to expel the *erotikà*, the *iupnotikà pathémata* I set myself in self-loathing to rewrite each page ten times, a hundred times over, striving every time to stuff it with fattier forcemeats . . . I, who dined this evening on a glass of milk. I had a reason for trying to use words to rival the bright-eyed peacock's tail, its aerial vanities; and what could it have been but the need to illumine with Bengal lights the floodstreams of the dark, the flowing black blood that laps the banks of Styx, over which, undrinking, I have leaned; the lava-ash greyness where, if I lost my sandal, it was only that I might return to the light; trepidant Empedocles I . . . ludicrous Cinderella.

Shall I recapitulate? Age about sixty, weight around eleven stone, senility just around the corner, underclothes smelling of carbolic. This evening, what's more, of Eau de Roche and sperm. In my wallet a credit card, an identity card, and booking No. 0034/B on the Etna Express. To my left, in the mattress, a still-warm hollow. She has only just left. Packaged on a stool to my right, my little purchases: an after-shave lotion, *Christ lag in Todesbanden* (Fischer Dieskau, baritone), a phial of Gardenal (got without a prescription).

I stop, look and listen to myself, give myself the once-over. A slow, an old man's pulse-rate (yesterday, catching a glimpse of the mercury, the high and low readings dangerously close together); the cartilages of a bat bled white; a rotten tooth in my top jaw throbbing steadily in time with the thudding pump of my heart. I take a look at my hands: on the backs of each, two or three brownish blotches the size of chickpeas, not there a few days ago. In my ears a ceaseless patter of rain, a scuffling of tiny feet, the hordes of termites patiently, perfunctorily, constructing the edifice of my death.

I try putting out the light. An infinitude of dots dances before me in the dark. Is this the Other, the Beyond of me? What an alphabet, blind man to blind man, how many runes to decipher! If only they would tell me my name, teach me who I am, and the meaning of this coil of time and space which I inhabit, and fail to assess with my wonky goniometries. I, with my bundle of hardened arteries, teeth in ruins, fungoid patches on my neck, varicose veins, and a mind bereft both of might and of madness . . . And worst of all, night and day, this pain, this fox at my vitals, here where I press my hand.

This, today – and take a good look at it – is the youngster of a hundred pages back.

All the same it was quite another, the gift I would have liked from the years: after so much lukewarm suffering, a week of consummate torment, a pinnacle to plummet from. And to go with a *Missa in angustiis* for the dying Dauphin, not this puling of a bum slung out of a bar. What I got instead were Threepenny Iliads, a laughable arena where this evening, crippled, backsliding warrior that I am, I struggle with a false god dressed as a cloud for the possession of a corpse.

Ah, words, you say . . . They haven't been enough, and never are. Not if every terror, the entirest, the direst, proliferates under my pen-nib in eel-whorls of ornament, in infamous trinities of adjectives; not if every slice of heart and sliver of entrail is translated for me, as it sees the light of day, into a corybantic uproar. Woe and alas, dear reader, my lone auditor and Aesculapius . . . and yet you guessed from the very start, my brother, my double, my faithful traitor, to whom I reach out beseechingly from these crumples of parchment. So why not own up to it? Writing has been, for me, merely a hollow mockery of living, a prosthesis of living. Every figure of speech has mimicked, and mimics, a scuffle of mercenaries, or a habit to be consummated in lavatorial seclusion.

Oh the sham, the shame, the shambles! . . . But there, reader, you have my head on a pikestaff. *Pourtant j'avais quelque chose là-dedans* . . .

LAST ASIDE

Prayer from the wings.

You then, meagre, mysterious life, what am I to say of you? Since you've always worn that air of a prinked-up doll, and never done a thing to persuade me that you're real . . . Loathsome-lovesome life! Pitiless, merciful . . . all right, get on with it! I have you now: a sword, an orange, a rose. Now I have you now I don't: a cloud, a breeze, an aroma.

Life . . . the more your fires dwindle the more I cherish them. Drop of honey, do not fall. Golden moment, do not leave me.